A Dog to Give Away

Also by Dr. Dave

A Dog to Give Away

Dr. Dave Perrin

Illustrations by
Carlos David González Rubio

Dave's Press Inc.

Published by Dave's Press Inc.
1521 Canyon-Lister Road
Creston, British Columbia
Canada V0B 1G2

Cover and book design by Warren Clark
Illustrations by Carlos David González Rubio
Edited by Elliott Cross
Printed and bound in Canada

Library and Archives Canada Cataloguing in Publication
Perrin, David, 1948-, author
    A dog to give away / Dr. Dave Perrin.
ISBN 978-0-9866569-7-2 (paperback)
    I. Title.
PS8631.E77625D64 2016   C813'.6   C2016-907204-5

Dedication

To:

Dr. Dave's grandchildren

James, Scarlet,

and those yet unborn

Acknowledgements

Every time I reach this final stage of completion for a book, I look back and wonder at the fact that I finally did it. Another book is going to print and it's time to offer thanks to those who assisted me in getting it there.

My first thank you goes to Lug. He was truly this man's best friend for many years and worthy of this small tribute to his memory. Many a night when things were not going as well as I would have liked, he listened to my words and gave me his furry shoulder to cry on. Neither man nor beast taught me more about love and devotion than Lug.

It always bothered me knowing that Lug had a history with another owner who no doubt missed him dearly when they were separated. Although I suspect he had led a pampered life before becoming lost, that was certainly not the case when he was making out on his own. Lug's terrible fear of even distant gunshot blasts and the sprinkling of shotgun pellets that showed up on subsequent X-rays over much of the left side of his body were evidence of that. He had obviously been the target of someone's ire at some point in time.

On any trip through an SPCA or Humane Society facility you will be met with dogs and cats staring out at you from behind the bars of their kennel. Each one of them has a story to tell. For some it is a story of mayhem and misery, or a story of a dear and caring owner passing on, while for others, like the hero of this book, it is a story of how they made a tragic mistake and ended up lost. You only have to listen to the radio, turn on the television or surf the internet to find stories of the same miseries in the lives of many humans who are lost and looking for a place of refuge. A recent trip to Indonesia where I witnessed firsthand the life of my guide, Rama Eudora, made me realize that many of our pets here at home have an easier life compared to people in the Third World.

I was terribly disappointed when my former editor Betsy Brierley was unable to come out of retirement to edit this book, but I was fortunate enough to find a great replacement in Elliott Cross. He has done a fantastic job in her stead, and I am thankful for his input. Wendy Liddle was unfortunately too busy to work her magic with the illustrations, but Carlos David González Rubio, an artist from Venezuela, appeared out of the ether of the internet to provide his services and add some color to my words. Thank you, Carlos. And, as always, Warren Clark has done a fantastic job with the design and layout of this book.

My final thanks go to the many readers and fans who have sent me emails of encouragement and nagged me at face to face appearances for new offerings. I hope Lug's story lives up to your expectations.

CHAPTER 1

Apollo could sense adventure in the air as he watched his owner sorting through the bags and boxes in the corner of the garage. He knew from previous experiences that whenever Jim started dragging out the tent, sleeping bags, and pack-boards they would be headed off on an outdoor adventure. He so loved it when his little family got out into the wilderness where he was allowed to run free and not be confined by a leash like he was here in the city. At the very thought of being out there, the big German Shepherd got so excited that he couldn't contain himself another second. Sidling over to the tall lean man who ruled his destiny, Apollo repeatedly nudged his nose under Jim's hand in the hopes of getting attention.

"You know what's coming, don't you buddy?" Jim put aside the sleeping bag that he had just dug out of the storage closet, sat down, and gave Apollo exactly what he was looking for – an enthusiastic pat and a rugged ruffling of the ears. "You're such a suck, Apollo. Don't you know that German Shepherds are supposed to be vicious guard dogs?"

Apollo stood there with a silly look on his face as Jim continued to stroke him and massage his ears. "Would you ever protect your dad if he needed your help?"

Paying absolutely no heed to the question, Apollo relaxed in the soft tone of his master's voice and the delightful stroking of his head.

"Well, enough of this," Jim said, grabbing one of the pack frames and securing a sleeping bag to the metal rack with bungee cords. "I need to get everything ready for tomorrow so we can have enough time to set up our camp before nightfall."

Apollo reluctantly wandered over to the corner of the garage and curled up where he could keep an eye on his master, who was busy stuffing cans and packages of dried food into the upper compartments of two backpacks. It was still light outside when Jim hefted them into the back of the old 4x4 that he used for his off-road camping trips.

Jim dug around in a grocery bag for a few seconds and produced an item that made Apollo snap to attention and jump to his feet. With his tail wagging and his eyes brimming with anticipation, he ran to check out Jim's clenched fist.

"You sure don't miss much, do you boy?"

Jim opened his hand and let the dog have the chunk of beef jerky. Apollo made short work of the small offering and nudged his master's hand in hope of more.

"That was just a treat…We'll save the rest for up on the mountain."

Apollo continued to stare expectantly at Jim as he sauntered to a hook on the garage wall and plucked off a long leather leash.

"Are you ready for your walk?"

Apollo yipped with excitement and twirled in circles in the center of the garage floor. That four-letter word always got his attention – how he loved to wander the streets with his master.

The rambunctious dog continued to dance around Jim as he stooped to connect the latch of the leash to the eye on the metal choke chain. Apollo would have loved more of that jerky, but going for a walk was definitely the next best thing.

The pair headed down the sidewalk past the corner store, the schoolyard, and all the other familiar places. As they sauntered along, Apollo stopped frequently to lift his leg and pee on lampposts. At others, he felt obligated to sniff intently to check for the scent of strange dogs in his neighborhood.

When they arrived at the park, there wasn't another human in sight, so Jim snapped off the leash and let Apollo run free. The moment he was released, Apollo tore off and began rooting through some underbrush beneath a clump of large maple trees. Dragging out a two-foot chunk of branch, he ran to his master and dropped it at his feet. Just as Jim was about to pick it up, Apollo grabbed it and took off.

"So you think you can keep it away from me, do you?"

Jim chased the dog around and around in circles, and only after he flopped puffing to the grass did Apollo drop the stick at his master's side.

It was almost dark when they arrived home. Barb had supper waiting on the table, and the smell of the beef stew made the big German Shepherd's mouth water. The moment his masters were seated at the table, Apollo moved to sit at the base of Jim's chair. Apollo knew from experience that this was the best place to be positioned in order to get tidbits from Jim's plate.

Apollo watched as his masters ate their meal and discussed the upcoming adventure.

"The boys at work couldn't stop talking about this lake," said Jim. "Kimberley's a pretty long haul, but if you get home right after work and I sneak away a few minutes early, we should be able to set up camp before dark."

Barb nodded. "It does sound fantastic, but it's a shame it has to be such a rushed trip. You know we both have to be at work Monday morning. Maybe we should have waited till we had more time."

Jim smiled at his wife. "You're such a worry wart. We'll check it out this weekend, and if it's as good as everyone says, we can go back for longer next time."

As their plates began to empty, Apollo crept closer and closer to Jim. Barb smiled as the dog gently nudged her husband's elbow and looked up at him expectantly.

"You and that dog." Barb smiled as Jim handed Apollo a big chunk of stew meat. "He so has you wrapped around his little pinkie."

"He doesn't have a little pinkie," Jim responded. "He just knows I'm a very generous man."

"He knows you're a big suck and that I won't feed him at the table," she responded. "But you just watch whose dog he is when it's time for me to decide what to do with the leftovers."

Barb was right…The moment the meal was over and she and Jim got up from the table, Apollo was there looking up at her with longing eyes as she scooped crunchies into his stainless steel dish and smothered it with the remainder of the stew and gravy from dinner.

Apollo was as ecstatic as ever when Barb arrived back at the house late the next afternoon. Barking enthusiastically, he danced in circles to welcome her. He hated the long days of waiting while his masters were away and he never really understood why, after just a short walk in the morning, they left him to sit and wait hours for their return.

As a pup, Apollo had been inventive with his time alone, and his masters had often been welcomed back home with long trails of toilet paper that stretched from one end of the house to the other, or chewed shoes that had been errantly left where only Apollo could find them. But all that fun came to an end when Jim brought home a big metal cage to confine Apollo and keep him from getting into trouble. It only took Apollo a couple of weeks to catch on, and after he had decided to give up his playful bad habits and behave himself, the cage was relegated to a corner of the garage.

"Come on…let's take you for a quick walk before Jim gets home." Barb clipped the clasp onto Apollo's collar and headed across the lawn to the sidewalk.

Apollo was disappointed that after only walking a couple of blocks on their normal route, Barb turned around and headed home. The moment she got back, she started rummaging in the kitchen and collecting things she was sure would be useful for the outing. By the time Jim got home, Barb had a pile of clothes, bags and plastic containers on the kitchen table.

"Are we all ready?" he asked.

"I think so," she replied. "I've got enough dog food for Apollo for a couple of days and lots of munchies for the drive in."

"Better grab a jacket or another sweater," Jim said. "It gets pretty chilly up in the high country this late in the summer."

Jim changed into his hiking boots, scooped some bags from the table, and headed outside. A few minutes later he had his old 4x4 out in the driveway waiting for Barb and Apollo to hop aboard. Barb ushered Apollo out of the house, locked the front door, and headed for the truck. The moment she opened the door and pushed her seat forward, Apollo climbed in and perched himself proudly on the back seat.

He loved this old truck. Here he was able to sit on his throne with the wind on his face and feel superior to all the other animals they drove by. When passing close to another dog, especially a big one, Apollo would bark aggressively to show that he was truly the king of this neighborhood.

After several hours on the open highway, Apollo drifted off to sleep with his head resting on the seat's armrest. He opened his eyes and perked up when they stopped at a traffic light in the little town of Kimberley, but drifted off again as soon as they were back on the highway. But the moment Jim turned off onto a dirt road, and geared the old truck down, Apollo immediately jumped to attention and stood up on the seat. He knew that when the going got slower and the road got bumpy they must be getting close to the place where he'd be able to run free and have fun. He craned his neck and watched attentively as they proceeded along a narrow roadway and crossed over a little bridge. He whined with anticipation when Jim pulled off to the side of the road and stared intently at a badly-weathered signpost.

"Is this the turn?" Barb asked.

Jim pulled out a scrap of paper from his jacket pocket and unfolded it on the dash beside him. "According to the map the boys drew me, this should be it."

Jim turned off onto the tributary that followed along the side of a marshy little lake. The lower portion of the narrow roadway was in pretty decent shape and Jim really pushed the old truck along.

Several times he had to back up and pull off onto a wider spot to allow another vehicle going in the other direction to pass. But as they drove on into the high country, there was little evidence that anyone had traveled there in the past few days. That suited Jim just fine, because he loved getting to places that few others chose to go.

They had driven for almost an hour when Jim pulled up and got out of the vehicle. A mudslide that had occurred some time during spring run-off had piled up dirt and boulders on the main portion of the road and eroded the edge of the bank. Apollo whined excitedly and offered to jump out of the truck.

"Stay, Apollo!" Jim yelled.

It wasn't often that his owner used this tone of voice with him, and he knew well enough to listen. Reluctantly, Apollo slowly sank to a sitting position and watched as Jim walked ahead of the truck.

"What do you think?" Barb asked.

Her husband returned to the truck and locked the front wheel hubs into four-wheel drive. "Other vehicles have passed over, so we should be okay."

Apollo leaned toward the center of the vehicle as his master engaged the four-wheel drive and crept slowly across the washout. Apollo was getting anxious; this drive was taking far longer than expected, and he kept hoping that soon he would be able to jump out and run free. On top of that, the farther they proceeded along the trail, the more rugged things got, and the slower they were able to drive.

The sun had sunk beneath the peek of a big pyramid-shaped mountain by the time the truck lumbered to a stop. Jim looked around uncertainly. The roadway ended in a small clearing, and there was nothing more than a narrow hiking trail that carried on. Apollo barked excitedly and spun around on his seat as Jim got out of the vehicle.

"I guess this is it," he said, and turned to Apollo. "Okay, okay… out you come."

Without waiting for another invitation, the big German Shepherd jumped to the ground over the side of the truck and started surveying the territory. With his nose to the rock-strewn surface, he ran in ever larger circles around the truck, relishing in the search for new, more wonderful aromas.

Jim stuck the keys for the truck beneath a boulder at the edge of the clearing. After hefting his pack onto his shoulders, he held the other one up while Barb slipped her arms through the straps and tightened up the buckles.

"We better get a move on," he warned. "We're running out of daylight." He was already starting down the trail when he stopped short and turned back to the truck.

"Apollo, come here." He stooped over and slapped his knees to encourage Apollo to quicken his pace. "Come here boy."

When Apollo came running up to him, Jim grasped the dog's choke chain and slipped it off over his head. Apollo gave him a bewildered look as his master tossed the collar onto the driver's seat of the truck.

"We sure don't want you getting hung up on some snag in the bush," Jim said.

Apollo stood looking up at the driver's seat of the truck for a moment, feeling like he had just lost something precious, but when Jim rushed to catch up with Barb, who was already hiking up the trail, he fell in line behind his masters.

By the time the threesome had made it to an open clearing next to a creek, darkness was upon them. There was a fire pit and a makeshift table left by people who had camped there before.

"Looks like where we're going to be spending the night," Jim said.

He and Barb hurriedly erected the tent. Then, while Jim set about making a fire, Barb readied their beds.

After lapping up cold water from the nearby stream, Apollo lay down to watch his masters' activities. He was captivated by the beam of light that zipped through the walls of the tent and darted about in the treetops as Barb unrolled the foam mattress pads and fluffed up their sleeping bags. Apollo's stomach growled, and he immediately focused his attention on Jim. His master already had smoke rising from the fire pit and flames were flickering at the twigs he had gathered and stacked together.

Apollo got up and wandered over to him. Giving Jim's elbow a nudge with his nose, he presented himself for attention.

"Getting hungry, aren't you boy?"

Apollo wagged his tail and stuck his nose under Jim's palm.

"You're not the only one…I'm pretty gaunt myself."

Jim and Barb had polished off a couple of bowls of steaming noodles and Apollo had eaten the last kernels of his dry dog food when Barb dragged out a package of wieners and began roasting them over the open fire. Apollo crept closer and closer to her and was finally rewarded with a cold wiener straight from the package. And when she passed a nicely blackened one over to Jim, he soon had a big dog sitting beside him watching every bite he took. And Apollo made sure he had the last bite.

After a brief sit around the campfire, it was bedtime, and the two-man tent became a two-person-plus-dog tent with Apollo moving restlessly from one side to the other and tramping on feet on every passage. Apollo was frequently awakened by unfamiliar sounds during the night. Of course he had to protect his masters and fend off whatever had made the noise by barking.

Jim left the tent at the break of day with Apollo glued to his heel. Within a few minutes, Jim had his fishing rod put together and was off to the creek with a Royal Coachman fly dangling from the end of his line. It wasn't long before he was hooting and hollering and dragging in little pan fries one after the other. Apollo was thrilled as he watched the little fish wriggle out of the water on the end of the line. He was even more elated to paw at them until they quit flopping when Jim took them off the hook and threw them on the bank.

By the time Barb crawled out of the tent, Jim was sitting on a log beside a roaring fire carefully watching over his fish as they curled up and sizzled in a pan full of butter. At his elbow, supervising his every move, was Apollo.

It was after ten before they were packed up and ready to move on. This campsite had been fine for one night, but Jim and Barb were determined to spend the next one camped on the lake.

The first part of the hike was like walking through a park. The trail meandered through a grassy, alpine meadow before following the creek as it tumbled from the lake above. Apollo was in heaven. He loved running back and forth through the open area, snuffing at marmot holes and trampling though the purple and yellow wild-flowers that grew everywhere. This was what he had been waiting for.

Apollo followed along behind Jim and Barb as they hiked alongside the creek, then turned to climb onto a steep, heavily-treed bench. The climb was difficult for his masters as they struggled over windfalls and stomped through boggy spots where their boots disappeared beneath the mud. Apollo found it much easier to just crawl under downed trees, and to him mud on his paws was no big deal.

As the terrain leveled off and came out into an open area at the top of the bench, his masters took off their packs and stretched out on the ground. While they rested, Apollo had time to slurp up water from a little spring and check out all the unusual scents. That's when he picked up a distinctive smell that he had never been exposed to before. With his nose to the ground he followed the scent to a thicket of brush on the edge of the clearing.

Suddenly there was a crashing of branches and a long-legged critter pounced out right in front of him. The sound of cracking tree limbs and the scent of the strange beast were so tantalizing that Apollo just couldn't resist. Determined to catch up, he ignored his owners' pleading calls and charged off after the peculiar critter.

The animal ran down a steep embankment with Apollo following close behind. Tearing through underbrush and leaping over downed trees, the animal made a desperate attempt to lose him. A number of times Apollo got within sight of this amazingly agile critter, only to have it melt into the surrounding landscape. Without any notion of what he would do if he caught up with it, Apollo charged on, until, totally exhausted, he fell panting to the ground.

It wasn't until he had rested somewhat that he even thought about where he was and what direction he had gone to get here.

The long-legged creature was long gone, and all Apollo wanted now was to be back with his owners.

He got up and looked to his left – all he could see was rock ledges and trees. He looked to his right – nothing but rock ledges and trees. He was lost.

CHAPTER 2

A pollo had been wandering for days. He was hungry and worried. Never before had he been away from his dear owners this long. Never before had he to wonder where his next meal would come from. Why had he taken off from them the way he had? It just seemed like he couldn't help himself. When that long-legged critter pounced out right in front of him, he just couldn't resist the temptation.

In the days after he had become lost, Apollo had spent hours circling around the rough terrain for some sign of his owners. Several times he thought he had caught their scent, but each moment of excitement had ended in disappointment. After a couple of days of fruitless searching, he had decided to start heading down the mountain. Surely then he would find the truck that had brought them to the end of that long and bumpy dirt road. Surely then he would find his owners.

Apollo followed a little stream without the slightest idea where it was leading him. After walking for most of the day, he stopped to lap up cool water as it flowed over a moss-covered log. Shaking his head, he pawed at a pesky mosquito that settled on his muzzle.

He was tired. Circling around and around on a small island of grass, he collapsed in a heap and licked absently at his paws. They were raw and sore from traveling over the rough, rocky terrain. Until a few days ago, the farthest he had walked at any one time had been the distance of a dozen city blocks, and even then it had been with a leather lead to keep him from going astray.

It was getting dark, and this was as good a place as any to spend the night. Curling up with his nose tucked into his tail, he lay with his head on his paws and closed his eyes. He dozed for about an hour before a noise woke him.

Was that what he thought it was? Perking his ears, he stood and focused his attention down the hill. Was that the sound of his owners calling him? It had to be! With one ear standing straight, and the other folded in its usual floppy state, he strained to hear beyond the tinkling of the water and the growling of his stomach. There it was again – the sound of a human voice. And there – the barking of a dog farther down the hill. Wagging his tail hopefully, Apollo waded across the stream and headed off through low-lying bushes. It was completely dark before he broke out of a thicket of trees and came upon an open field.

Approaching the area cautiously, he sniffed the air, hopeful for the familiar scents of home. There were indeed lots of smells, but none reminiscent of the house he had been raised in. He stopped before a barrier of steel wires that stretched as far as he could see in either direction. He extended his nose to sniff at the obstruction, but recoiled with a yelp when the wire erupted in sparks and an electric shock jolted his body. He panicked and fled into the brush and settled behind a clump of birch trees.

He was still there when light began filtering through the trees. Cautiously, he crept on his belly toward the steel wires. As terrified as he was of them, the growling of his stomach, and the haunting feeling of loneliness, convinced him he had to cross beyond them.

He peered in the direction he was sure he had heard a human voice the night before, and carefully made his way alongside the wires. Four-legged beasts munched at grass in the field below him. Apollo had passed animals like this before when his owners had taken him on weekend walks in the country. He knew he was to have nothing to do with them, because whenever he had shown interest in them in the past, his owners had jerked on his lead and shouted, "No!"

Apollo followed the wires until he found a spot where the ground dipped and the bottom wire continued straight. Crouching low, and laying his ears flat to his head, he crawled beneath the bottom wire, trying desperately not to touch it again. He got under without incident, and was partway across the field when the four-legged beasts spotted him. A little brown one, with a white tail and spotted face, bawled in panic and ran off in the opposite direction, while a big one with long curly horns tossed its head and galloped straight toward him.

In a state of total panic, Apollo ran in the direction of a tall white building where he was sure he had heard human voices and a barking dog the night before, hoping that there he would find safety. He barged into a yard surrounded by wooden rails and tore at full tilt past a log building. Big white-and-brown birds scattered in all directions at his approach, making terrified clucking sounds as they flapped their wings and took flight.

Apollo slowed to a trot and looked around furtively. He must be close to the place where people lived. Maybe here he would find his owners.

"Yah…Get outta here, you chicken-chasing cur!"

Apollo turned with a start as a portly man ran toward him. Waving a rake high above his head, he hollered, "Rover! Spike! Sic him!"

The big German Shepherd was already running by the time he heard the yipping of the two dogs behind him. As big as he was, Apollo had little experience with defending himself against other

animals. His owners had always been quick to intercede whenever another dog had come after him.

Apollo tore past a tall white farmhouse and down a dirt road. In the distance, he could still hear the voice of the angry man egging his dogs on, "Sic him boys! Sic him! Get that mutt outta here!"

It was several minutes later before Apollo dared to slow and take a worried look over his shoulder. The two shaggy brown mutts had stopped their chase at the farm gate, and Apollo could no longer hear the voice of the angry man with the rake. His chest heaved as he struggled for breath. Crossing over a ditch at the side of the road, Apollo collapsed behind a clump of alders where he had a good view of the road. His long pink tongue dangled to the point where it was almost touching the ground.

What was going on? When he had been with his owners, humans had always been kind to him; they had always extended their hands in gestures of friendship. Never had a man threatened him like this one had today.

With his head resting on his paws, Apollo lay there puffing for well over an hour. Several times he jumped to his feet for fear that Rover, Spike, or the angry man with the rake were descending upon him. How could life have changed so drastically in just a few days?

Apollo was still exhausted when he reluctantly struggled to his feet and wandered farther down the dirt road. All he could think of was putting distance between himself and the angry man and his dogs. Apollo's throat was parched from panting; he was in desperate need of water. He trotted round a corner, and there, far below him, was a frothing ribbon of water tumbling down the mountain. Slowly, one step after the other, he worked his way the length of the steep, rocky bank, waded into the stream, and collapsed. Lapping at the cool refreshing liquid, he lay there totally submerged with just his head sticking out and his long fluffy tail flowing behind him in the stream.

Apollo was shivering before he pulled himself out of the water and began picking his way up the embankment. He was refreshed now, but also ever more conscious of the terrible grumbling in his tummy. As he clambered onto the roadway, he imagined his owners filling his big steel bowl to the brim with dog food and plunking it down on the kitchen floor in front of him. In his current state, he wouldn't even have waited for the tidbits from Jim's supper before diving into his meal.

Apollo was wandering down the center of the road, drooling at the thought of munching his kibbles, when an old gray truck rattled round the bend and headed straight for him. At the last moment, the driver leaned on the horn and swerved to miss him. Terrified by the near miss, Apollo leaped over the ditch and ran into the bushes. The shrill blaring of the horn echoed through the narrow draw as the truck tore past.

CHAPTER 3

For days Apollo wandered back and forth along dirt roads in search of something he recognized. The humans here lived on little patches of ground that had been carved out of the bush, and every time Apollo tried to check things out, he was yelled at by humans or chased away by resident dogs.

How different it was from the towns he had lived in – no long ribbons of hard white concrete where his owners had walked him, no flashing lights where they would stop for cars to pass, no short grass for him to trot on, and very few houses where potential two-legged benefactors could be found. Here there was only long, wild grass, trees and scraggly brush.

Apollo so wanted to get back to his loving owners again, but had no idea of even what direction he had to travel to find them. At the moment the sole focus of his life was to find something, anything, to eat. From experience he knew that all food originated from the hands of humans. His owners had taught him to refuse offerings from strangers, but now he would be willing to take almost anything from anyone. He was so hungry that all he could think about was putting an end to the horrible rumblings emanating from his belly.

In desperation, Apollo chomped on long blades of grass

growing on the side of the road. He struggled to swallow, and choked as the coarse, unpalatable mass got caught in the back of his throat. Gagging reflexively, he retched it back up. Determined to put something in his belly, however, he chewed it again and again until he finally forced it down his throat.

Following the edge of the dirt road, with his nose close to the ground, Apollo continued searching for anything that could satisfy his unbearable hunger. As he rounded a bend, he caught scent of something that reminded him of home. He circled around, sniffing with more and more certainty. There it was, just over the bank – a bag with something inside it. Excitedly, he climbed over and grabbed it. Stepping on one end, he tore madly through the plastic with his teeth. The dried remnants of a sandwich disappeared in a flash. Wanting to get every last morsel from the inside of the bag, Apollo licked crazily at the slippery plastic surface. He knew well the smell of the sticky substance that stuck the two pieces of bread together: Jim used to smear a gob of the pasty brown stuff on the roof of Apollo's mouth with his finger and laugh as the dog licked madly to try and swallow it.

Rounding a corner, Apollo came upon a wide open area of short grass that stretched as far as he could see. Excited that it looked similar to the park Jim used to take him to, he quickened his pace. Could this be the place where Jim would throw sticks again and again for him to retrieve?

With his nose to the ground, Apollo trotted first one way then another, searching for something he recognized. He mounted a small plateau where fine grass was clipped short to the ground and a pole with something waving on the top stuck out of a hole in the ground. He was about to lift his leg and mark his territory on the pole, when a little white ball fell from the sky and landed next to him. He trotted over as the ball rolled to a stop. He sniffed at the ball and picked it up in his mouth.

"Hey you, get away from my ball!"

Startled, Apollo dropped the ball and whirled in the direction of the voice. A little cart with two men aboard came whizzing over a knoll toward him. One of the men was holding a stick in his hands and swinging it wildly in his direction.

"Get out of here! A golf course is no place for a dog!"

Apollo took off in a panic with his ears flat to his head and his tail streaming behind him. He ran until he found a gulley where a stream cut through the short grass. He lapped at the water as it flowed past him, then collapsed in the deep grass where no one could see him. Why were the humans all so mean to him now? He had always tried to do what his owners asked of him, and never before had he feared that people might hurt him.

He lay there for the rest of the day, watching from a safe distance as humans carrying long sticks and riding in whizzing carts went back and forth either side of him. Time and again, little white balls fell from the sky close to him and humans poked in the grass above him. Each time, he lay there motionless until the danger passed.

It was dark when Apollo finally crept out of his hiding place and ventured back into the open. The humans with their long sticks and whizzing carts had seemingly departed. Wandering back and forth across the short grass area, Apollo continued searching for something to fill his growling belly.

The night was quiet, but every once in a while he heard a human voice echo in the distance. There it was again – a man's laughter. Apollo tipped his head and perked his upright ear in the direction of the sound. Over there – where the sound of an engine roared to life and the lights of a car blinked on.

As much as his fear of humans was growing ever more pronounced, Apollo still associated them as his only source of sustenance. Therefore, fearful but determined, he trotted toward the sound that promised to end his hunger.

He slowed as he neared a cluster of buildings and circled around the area to check them out. One of them had the intense smell of fumes, just like the old vehicle that his owners had driven in. He crept on through the shadows to a place where the whizzing buggies that he had seen on the short grass were congregated. They were quiet now. Apollo lifted his nose into the air and his heart beat ever faster. Food. He could smell food! It was coming from that big building where all the people were chatting.

Slinking through the night, Apollo circled round the building. Out on a balcony and on the other side of some windows, he could see people sitting at tables and eating. His stomach growled intensely at the sight, and it brought back memories of all the times he had sat and watched his owners eat, knowing full well that before long he too would find out how great the food tasted.

Again and again, Apollo sniffed the air, certain that the food was close, probably near the back of the building. He skulked nearer, then crept slowly up a flight of stairs that took him closer to where he was sure the smell was coming from. The activity on the other side of a door – the sizzling sounds of food, the clatter of dishes – reminded Apollo of home, of the many times he had sat hopefully waiting for a few tidbits to be dropped in his direction.

Long ropes of drool hung from the side of Apollo's mouth as he anticipated actually getting something to eat. His eyes widened as he spotted a bucket filled to the brim with heavenly-smelling treats, almost like his owners had left them there for him. Apollo started by licking the great-tasting liquid at the top, then dug deeper to where different colored vegetables and scraps of meat were all mashed together. He was so engrossed in driving his snout deep into this fantastic feast that he tipped the bucket over and sent it crashing down the stairs.

A fat man in a white apron threw open the screen door and hollered, "Yah, get outta here, you good fur nothin' mutt!"

Waving his arms, the fat man continued his tirade, yelling now at the slender young fellow who followed him onto the porch. "Justin, how many times have I told you to put the scraps in the garbage can and secure the lid?" The fat man shook his fist in anger and stared into the darkness into which the dog had retreated. "Look at the mess it made!" He pointed to the trail of slop that now covered the stairs. "At least it wasn't a bear like the last time you couldn't do as you were told. Now clean it up!"

Apollo watched from the shadows as Justin grabbed a shovel and dutifully slogged to the bottom of the stairs to retrieve the bucket. Moving slowly and deliberately, he scraped everything back into the container. He whistled softly to keep his boss from hearing, and then, in a low voice, called out, "Here boy, here boy." He walked to the base of a tree on the edge of the course and dumped the bucket. "You better clean this up boy, or I'll be in even more trouble tomorrow."

Apollo stayed motionless behind some shrubs until long after the noises from the building had diminished. Only then did he creep to the base of the tree where Justin had deposited the food scraps. Apollo ate until his tummy was so full that he couldn't swallow another bite. Satisfied for the first time in days, he curled up and fell asleep.

Apollo was awakened by the sound of a machine as it passed him by. The human perched on top of it never noticed Apollo, and the machine continued on, spitting short pieces of grass in its wake. Staying in place long after the machine had passed from sight, Apollo rose cautiously and nibbled at the last fragments of food that he had missed in the dark, then licked at the grass until all of the tasty flavor was gone. With his belly still full to near bursting, his thoughts returned to his owners and his need to search for home.

CHAPTER 4

Over the next few days, Apollo developed a routine of hiding in the long grass and trees during the day and sneaking back to the building where people ate after dark. Every night, Justin snuck out at the end of his evening shift to deposit food scraps at the base of the same tree he had used the first night. Several times, he stood staring into the darkness with meat in hand trying to coax Apollo out of the shadows. And although the dog was tempted to trust this friendly human, he remained out of sight. Only when all was quiet did Apollo sneak out and see what Justin had left for him.

One night Apollo was lying behind some shrubs just beyond sight of his feeding tree, when Justin climbed down the stairs and started walking in his direction with bucket in hand. Apollo was brimming with anticipation of another tasty meal.

Justin was almost to the feeding tree when the door opened again and the fat man bellowed, "Justin, have you been feedin' leftovers to that darned mutt?!"

Justin stopped dead in his tracks and returned to the back stairs. "I just leave him a few scraps now and then," he responded timidly. "The poor thing looked so hungry."

"Well, it's time for you to make up your mind which one of

you is goin' to go hungry. Because if you don't put an end to your foolishness right now, you can find yourself another job. The course manager stopped by this morning to ask if we were feeding that cur, and I told him we weren't. He doesn't want a dog crapping all over the fairways, and he's afraid the mutt may go crazy and attack someone."

Apollo watched as Justin climbed the stairs, emptied the bucket into a big dumpster, and followed the fat man inside. Apollo could hear the fat man ranting on, "Some days, Justin, I swear you must leave your brain at home when you come to work."

The moment the door closed and the lights blinked out, Apollo crept to the base of the feeding tree and sniffed for supper. But there was nothing there. And when he returned the following day, hoping for the feedings to resume, he was again disappointed.

It was still too early in the morning for the whizzing buggies or the humans with long sticks to be on the short grass, so Apollo felt safe as he left the treed area behind the restaurant and ventured into the open. He was heading to the ravine where he could hide out for the day, when he heard the sound of one of the grass-throwing machines approaching. He was already running when the operator spotted him. Leaving his planned route, the man sped up his machine and drove right toward Apollo.

"Yah…go away!" he hollered.

Apollo ran for all he was worth toward a treed section in the distance. Only after he dove into the bushes and could no longer hear the machine behind him did he stop running.

Apollo lay there for hours trying to make up his mind what to do next. He so wanted to be able to find his way back home, but he still hadn't the slightest idea which way he would have to go to get there. Now that Justin was no longer able to provide for him, there was no reason to stay here. The familiar rumbling in his tummy had returned, and along with it the feeling of desperation. The only

thing that made sense to him was to keep wandering until he found something that looked familiar. And with that in mind Apollo got up and headed off through the underbrush.

He had been wandering for most of the day when he detected a strange scent on the breeze. He had been following a narrow trail through the forest in the hope that it would lead him somewhere safe, somewhere with food, and somewhere without angry humans. Stopping, he lifted his nose high, and sniffed the air. What was that smell? It was a mixture of so many scents that he couldn't separate them into something that he recognized. Lowering his head to the ground, he started trotting in the direction of the smell. He had to find out what it was, but even though he hoped food was involved, he was certain that something wasn't quite right.

Apollo slowed, then stopped abruptly when he saw movement on the trail ahead. He stared at something that was hanging from a branch on some bushes ahead, moving back and forth in the breeze.

Walking hesitantly toward it, he saw yet another and another in trees farther on. He sniffed absently at the limp structure – it was the same clear material that his owners had used to surround the food they stored for later use.

As Apollo continued along the trail, he saw these limp things everywhere, and the aroma of the strange place became so intense it was overwhelming. He slowed to a near crawl as he came to an opening at the end of the trail where trees and brush gave way to freshly upturned earth and a tremendous assortment of debris scattered in disorganized heaps. He stopped and stared suspiciously at his new surroundings. Standing like a statue at the edge of the woods, he struggled to convince himself it was safe to explore this strange place further. All was quiet except for the cawing of a few big black birds that hopped randomly from place to place in the rubble. Apollo watched as they picked things up, tipped their heads back, and gobbled them down. These birds were obviously finding things to eat. So maybe he'd find something as well.

After several minutes of cautious observation, Apollo ventured onto the upturned dirt and crept out into the center of the open area. With his nose close to the ground, he wandered until the smell of something interested him. He stopped and pawed through a jumble of debris until he flipped out a container filled to the brim with a stinky mixture of meat and decaying vegetables. He wolfed it down and licked the container clean.

While rummaging through some other scattered rubbish, he was disturbed by the sound of an approaching vehicle. Terrified of yet another encounter with an angry human, Apollo ran back to the trail he had previously followed, and dropped to the ground out of sight.

The black birds scattered with squawks of complaint as a man got out of his car, went round to his trunk and tossed out boxes of trash. Within minutes, he hopped back in his car and drove away.

As soon as the vehicle had gone from sight and the sound of the engine had faded, Apollo crept out of his hiding place and trotted over to the recently discarded material. The birds had gotten there before him and issued shrieks of complaint as he approached and began pawing through the newly presented offerings.

Apollo had torn open a big black bag filled with all sorts of interesting tidbits, when he sensed a very different feeling in his belly. It was still rumbling and complaining, but now he no longer felt hungry. Now he felt sick.

He continued to paw through the material in the bag, and even ate several morsels, but after a few minutes he sauntered back to the shelter of the trees, leaving the spoils to the big black birds.

Apollo lay there motionless. For the first time in days, he was no longer interested in food. All he wanted was for the horrible feeling of nausea to go away. Getting up, he shifted his body from side to side, then stood staring straight ahead with his head hanging. Drool dangled from the corners of his mouth. He gagged several times, wanting to expel whatever was making him feel so terribly sick, then lay down with his eyes closed and his head on his paws.

That's when the vomiting began. Again and again Apollo threw

up the food that just moments before had seemed his salvation. When he finally finished retching, he lay there completely unable to move. He felt so tired; tired of constantly looking for his next meal; tired of not knowing where to look for his owners; tired of being an outcast. Stretched out on his side, Apollo lay there quietly with his eyes closed, not caring what went on around him.

Vehicles came one after the other throughout the rest of the day to this place of refuse. Although he could hear the racket of humans discarding debris from the backs of their cars and trucks, Apollo lay there totally dejected, not moving a muscle. Maybe this was where a reject like him truly belonged: here with the cast-offs from human lives and the big black birds who continued their incessant cawing and chattering. Darkness fell, and still the dog did not stir.

It was only when light began filtering through the trees that Apollo lifted his head and rolled onto his tummy. He felt terrible, and when he struggled to his feet on trembling legs, he battled to hold his head up to look around. What should he do? Where should he go? What hope was there for a homeless dog without anyone to care for him?

Apollo turned and staggered toward the place of the upturned earth. It was early morning, and as yet there was no sign of the humans. Apollo took jagged steps toward the center of the dump site and was almost to the place where he had found his last meal, when he saw movement from the corner of his eye.

Apollo's eyes widened and his heart thumped wildly as he focused on a new source of danger. What was that big black creature rummaging through the boxes and bags at the far corner of the dump site? Apollo lifted his head and stared in awe – he had never seen such a creature before. Sniffing the air, he detected a scent far more pungent than any other in the smorgasbord of odors emanating from this vile place.

The creature stopped foraging and focused his attention on Apollo. For almost a minute, both animals continued to stare at one another across the tangled jungle of debris. The big black creature sniffed the air again and again, then stood on his haunches like a two-legged human and stared in Apollo's direction.

Apollo stood stock-still until the creature returned to all fours and began moving toward him. A low rumble emitted from Apollo's throat as the creature got closer and closer. Apollo began to back away as the brute advanced. When the creature was just twenty feet away, Apollo half turned and yipped in panic. The big black creature huffed sharp bursts of air in and out and stared intently at Apollo. It stopped for a few seconds, then advanced in rapid, sharp bursts, slapping the ground in front of it with its massive paws. Apollo ran in a panic down the trail that had led him to this infernal place. He was a long way down the path before he dared to slow and peer back over his shoulder. It appeared that the creature had stopped, apparently content to chase away an invader from its feeding ground.

Apollo continued his retreat until he could run no more. When he came upon a trickling stream, he collapsed with his muzzle immersed in the cool liquid. Between gasps for breath, he lapped the water until he had quenched his thirst. Rising on trembling limbs, he looked warily around him. Satisfied that he was safe for the moment, he followed the tiny stream a short distance and curled up under some bushes.

CHAPTER 5

Apollo lay stretched out on his side for the remainder of that day and part of the next before stirring from his place of rest. Finally, several hours after the sun had risen, he hoisted himself onto shaky legs and cautiously made his way back to the trickling stream and the puddle of water where he had initially quenched his thirst. He stood staring down the trail in the direction that he had fled, before stooping to drink.

Everything in this strange place was so complicated. When he had been with his owners, they had always decided what he was to do and when he was to do it. Only once, when they had brought him to that horrible place with the metal cages where he had had things done to his sore ear, had he been forced to go without food and water for more than a few hours.

Apollo knew he had to find a source of food again, even though his belly seemed to suggest that it wasn't yet interested. He was very weak and couldn't go much longer without sustenance. Uncertain as to which direction to go, he stood on the trail for several minutes looking first one way then the other. He stared down the trail in the direction from which he came — he was not the least bit interested in another confrontation with the big black creature. He looked the other way – the humans from the place with the short grass would not want to see him again either.

Abandoning the trail, Apollo took off in an entirely new direction. Maneuvering around a clump of alders, he struggled over a windfall and pushed through thick underbrush. Without the slightest inkling of where he was going, he wandered aimlessly through the forest, wading through bogs and pushing under thorn bushes that tore at his flesh.

After an hour of walking, Apollo lay his tired body down beneath a big pine tree and rested his chin on his paws. He closed his eyes and took a nap. He awoke and was about to get up and carry on his journey, when a big bird with several smaller ones

following in its wake landed only a few feet from him on the other side of some bushes. Apollo watched attentively as the birds pecked at the ground in front of them, and he waited quietly as they continued to feed only a short distance away.

At first, Apollo never even considered the possibility that these birds could be a source of food – after all, he had never killed anything in his life. But as he watched the birds get closer, his muscles began to tremble with excitement and the tip of his tail twitched ever so slightly. Rising slowly, he crept closer and closer. He opened his mouth and pounced.

There was a flurry of activity as all but one of the flock of birds panicked and flew off. The one that remained wriggled and screeched as Apollo held it firmly in his grasp. Only after several quick chomps of his jaw did the bird rest quietly in his mouth.

Apollo dropped the lifeless bird and sniffed at it curiously, still not really thinking of it as food. But once he licked at a wound on the bird's breast and tasted blood, that all changed, and by the time he journeyed on, all that remained of his prey was a scattering of gray feathers.

Apollo traveled only a short while longer before emerging into a clearing. He stopped. Sniffing the air, he stared uncertainly at the human dwelling before him. It was a little log house with a rickety shed in the backyard. In the distance, Apollo could see several other houses. This was obviously a place where many more humans lived.

Apollo lay down and focused patiently on the scene before him. Although he couldn't see any signs of activity, he was terrified of further human conflict. He would wait until dark to venture in for a closer look. He had proven that he could provide for himself in some small ways, but he still thought of humans as the source of his necessities.

It was twilight by the time a car pulled up to the little house and an old woman with long gray hair walked inside and clicked on an outside light. Apollo waited attentively for signs of further activity. After dark, the old woman came out of a back door and started calling, "Here, Lass…here Lass."

Apollo stood up and snuck closer as he saw a shaggy collie come out of the shed and plod slowly in the old woman's direction. "Come girl…come girl…come get your supper."

Apollo began to drool. The sound of those words was so similar to the ones his owners had used just before feeding him. Wriggling between the drooping strands of barbed wire that surrounded the perimeter of the yard, he inched nearer to the house. When the old woman went back inside, Apollo skulked across the short grass to where the shaggy old dog lay munching her bowl of food.

She looked up at him as he approached, whined uncertainly, and took a few steps back from her supper. Emitting a low-pitched rumble from deep in his throat, Apollo lowered his head and advanced toward the old dog's bowl. He gulped down the contents, slowing only when he coughed while gagging down a mouthful of dry kernels.

Lass passively laid back and watched as Apollo devoured her food and licked the bowl clean. The moment he finished eating, Apollo slunk off into the darkness where he would be safe from the old woman. For the first time in days, Apollo felt content as he drifted off to sleep.

Over the next few weeks, Apollo developed a routine of patrolling the neighborhood in search of sustenance. He had found a house on the very same road where brown birds far bigger than the one he had eaten in the woods were kept. He had discovered how much fun it was to chase one down then carry it off to eat in the bush.

Every night Apollo showed up at the log house at dusk. The old woman was so predictable in her feeding habits that stealing at least some of the food put out for Lass was easy. As each night passed without incidence, Apollo got more brazen and waited less time before coming out in the open. One evening, he was halfway through gulping down the contents of Lass's bowl, when the back door to the log house opened and a shrill voice screeched, "Yaah! Get out of here! What do you think you're doing stealing poor Lass's food?"

Kernels flew in all directions as Apollo jerked to attention and fled the scene. He was already near the fence when he turned to see the old woman standing next to Lass with a broom held high overhead. Diving through the drooping wires of the barbed wire fence, Apollo ran till he reached the covering canopy of the surrounding forest. What was he to do? He had finally found another reliable source of food, and now this!

When Apollo returned to the log house the following night, he was disappointed to see the old woman sitting on her back stoop. Crouching behind some bushes, Apollo watched with drool hanging from his jowls as Lass slowly picked away at her food. Only after the old collie had finished eating and the old woman had retreated into the house, did Apollo squeeze through the barbed wire fence and guardedly pick his way across the backyard.

He had just stuck his muzzle into the bowl to vacuum up the few remaining kernels, when the door to the log house flew open and the old woman rushed at him with the broom held high. "Yaah! Get out of here, you useless mutt!"

Lass struggled to her feet at the excitement and gave her owner a few feeble woofs of defiant support as Apollo bolted down the driveway and out onto the road.

When he recovered from his panic and quit running, he found himself near the house with the big brown birds. Skulking along the ditch on the edge of the roadway, he poked his head over the brim of the trench and surveyed the yard. The brown birds were now loitering about in a pen that was completely surrounded by wire. Apollo stood transfixed, watching as they waddled back and forth and pecked casually at the ground. He crept up the bank, focusing entirely on the birds. Catching and eating one when he was hungry was a bonus, but it was the thrill of the chase that now enticed him most. He was at the fenced-in enclosure before the birds spotted him and started a commotion. Whining with excitement at the prospect of another chase, Apollo stood up on his hind legs and pawed at the wire. The more the birds squawked and flew erratically about the enclosure, the more excited he became. He was leaping frantically against the wire when he heard the blast and felt a terrible burning sensation along his back and left hind leg. He fell to the ground, then struggled to his feet. He was sprinting to the roadway when he heard the second blast.

CHAPTER 6

Apollo limped to a canopy of shrubs above the log house. As much as he would have liked to get farther from the humans, he was in so much pain that he stopped the moment he was out of sight. Unable to sleep, he continually flexed and extended his left hind leg, licking at the blood that oozed from a multitude of puncture wounds. Although his constant discomfort was his main focus of attention, his mind kept flashing back to the horrible loud bang that caused the searing pain in his leg. He never wanted to hear that sound again.

By the end of the third day, Apollo's hunger overcame his reluctance to move. Dragging himself from his lair, he limped to his viewpoint above the log house and waited. For hours all was quiet with no sign of either Lass or the old woman. Just as daylight was beginning to fade, a car pulled up in front of the house. The old woman got out of the car and made her way into the house.

Apollo crept through the barbed wire fence and lay behind a margin of tall grass at the edge of the property. His stomach growled in anticipation. He waited expectantly as darkness fell and long slivers of light diffused from the windows of the log house into the backyard. He was beginning to wonder if he would go hungry again tonight, when the back door opened and the old woman stepped onto the back stoop. Apollo instinctively tensed when he saw her and took a hesitant step onto the short grass.

"Here Lass, here Lass, here Lass."

When there was no indication that the old dog was coming, the old woman walked toward the shed yelling even louder. "Lass! Come Lass…it's time to eat!"

Apollo watched expectantly as Lass finally appeared and hobbled in her owner's direction. "There's a girl," the old woman chirped, setting down the bowl and tenderly stroking the old dog's head. "You poor thing. You're moving slower every day, and now you're even having trouble hearing me."

Apollo watched attentively as the old woman retreated into the house. Waiting till Lass lay down to begin picking at her food, he crept through the darkness while keeping an eye on both the back door and the bowl of food. The moment Lass saw him approach, she struggled to her feet, backed away from her supper, and watched passively as the bigger dog demolished her meal and licked the bowl clean. The moment he had finished, he limped back up the hill and returned to his lair.

This state of affairs went on for weeks, with Apollo stealing from Lass whenever the opportunity presented itself. The pain from his wounds had all but faded and his entire focus in life now became satisfying his hunger. Sometimes the old woman sat on her back stoop the entire time that Lass ate her food, and on those nights Apollo went hungry. Other times, Lass was quicker to dive into her food, leaving far less for Apollo to steal. The night before, Lass had eaten more than half her food before he had gotten to it, and Apollo had decided that tonight he wasn't going to let that happen again. He was halfway down the hill by the time the old woman had retreated into the house and closed the back door. He rushed toward the bowl. Aggressively pushing Lass aside, Apollo began gulping down the dry kernels of dog food.

"Get out of here, you dirty mutt!" The old woman was almost upon him. With her broom held high and her long gray hair hanging in her eyes, she lunged toward him. Apollo turned to flee just as the broom thumped the ground in the exact spot he had just vacated.

"How many times am I going to have to chase you away?!" the old woman screeched. "I'm sick and tired of you tormenting us!"

For the next two days, the old woman sat on her stoop staring up the hill until Lass had finished her meal. On the third day, Apollo was in his usual spot at the top of the hill waiting to see what would happen with his dinner when a strange-looking car pulled into the driveway. A man wearing a pointy cap and pants with a stripe down the leg opened the car door and sauntered toward the log house. Apollo heard a knock and shortly after the high-pitched voice of the old woman. As the humans walked to the backyard near the old shed, Apollo could hear the old woman talking in a voice that grew louder and louder.

"He'll come out here tonight I tell you! He just waits up there on the hillside until I put out Lass's food, and the moment I'm out of sight he rushes down to steal it from her. He's a brazen devil that dog! The neighbor caught him killing chickens and filled his butt with buckshot, but that didn't seem to slow him down much."

The man responded in a calm voice, "I know this situation has you worked up, Mrs. Royson, but the RCMP have more important things to do than chase stray dogs around the countryside."

"I've called the municipal office in Nelson, and they tell me that it's part of your duties in rural areas!" Mrs. Royson retorted. "And I'll be calling your office a dozen times a day to get you to do your duty if that's what it'll take."

The policeman sighed and shook his head ruefully. "What do you expect me to do, run around in the dark with a flashlight looking for a delinquent dog?"

"Well someone better think of something!" Mrs. Royson shouted at him. "Go up to the fence and look. I bet he's there right now watching us. I'll feed Lass, and we can watch from the house. He'll come…I know he will."

Apollo watched suspiciously as Mrs. Royson carried the food bowl into the backyard and began calling. "Come Lass, come Lass, there's a girl."

Apollo drooled as the humans retreated onto the back stoop and into the house, and old Lass lay down to start eating her supper. Apollo stood up, took a few steps in her direction, then stopped and sniffed the air. Something just didn't feel right. Reluctantly, he retreated to beyond the tall grass and watched suspiciously from a distance.

Lass had finished her food and returned to her bed in the shed when the door opened and Mrs. Royson and the policeman walked into the backyard.

"He's a devil dog that one!" Mrs. Royson bellowed. "He just wanted to make a liar out of me!"

Apollo squeezed through the barbed wire and withdrew into the bush when the policeman clicked on his flashlight and headed in his direction.

"Just look around up there," Mrs. Royson called after him. "He has a hard-packed trail tramped down, and a spot where he always lays and watches me."

But by the time the policeman reached Apollo's viewpoint, the dog was long gone.

CHAPTER 7

With his regular source of food in jeopardy once again, Apollo had to change his habits and travel farther from his lair in search of sustenance. He wandered down the road to the neighboring yard, and watched expectantly as the big brown birds strutted about in their enclosed run. He drooled and his tail twitched involuntarily at the thought of catching one, but he never climbed the bank or ventured closer. The fear of the loud bang and the searing pain of his last encounter was still fresh in his memory. He wandered about in this strange little community from one backyard to another, finding tidbits here and there, but he was never able to put an end to the terrible rumbling in his tummy.

For more than a week he showed up at the top of the hill below his lair with the hope of sharing Lass's food, but Mrs. Royson always stayed on her back stoop waiting patiently for Lass to finish her dinner.

One night, when Apollo was almost ready to give up and move on, there was a change in Mrs. Royson's activity. As usual, Apollo showed up hungry and tired from a long day of fruitless scavenging. He watched expectantly as Mrs. Royson went about her routine. Calling Lass, she put the bowl down in front of the old dog, and then, to Apollo's dismay, she walked up the hill toward him.

"Come boy…come boy," she called in the same quiet soothing voice she used with Lass.

Apollo watched warily till Mrs. Royson was halfway up the hill, then he turned in panic and disappeared into the darkness.

Hours later, when all the lights from the house were extinguished, Apollo crept back to the top of the hill to check things out. When he could see no sign of Mrs. Royson, nor pick up her scent, he inched down the hill to where he had last seen her. And there, to his surprise, was a bowl of food.

Taking one last look around, he gobbled it down, sparing hardly enough time to breathe between bites. With his belly full once again, he returned to his lair and slept peacefully through the rest of the night.

Night after night, Mrs. Royson repeated the same procedure. Walking up the hill, she would call, "Here boy…here boy," and extend the bowl of food in his direction. Each night, Apollo stayed just out of sight, only coming to feed after Mrs. Royson had set the bowl down and left. On one occasion, he let her get close enough to see him and extend her hand in his direction before he retreated into the darkness.

The following night, Mrs. Royson never called to him; she only set the bowl on the ground halfway down the hill. For several more nights in a row, she repeated the same procedure, leaving the bowl closer and closer to where she fed old Lass. After several more nights, she tied Lass to the back stoop and left Apollo's bowl right inside the door to the shed where Lass usually slept.

Apollo approached his dinner warily, barely able to see his dish in the faint light coming from the log house. Stopping and watching for long periods of time, he crept slowly into the shed. He ate sporadically, constantly looking over his shoulder for fear of being trapped, then fled as quickly as he could.

This went on for over a week until Apollo was more confident about accepting his food in the enclosure. On several occasions, he even laid down to enjoy his meal more. He quit fidgeting and never really noticed that each night his bowl was placed farther from the door and closer to the far end of the shed.

He had just begun eating his dish of food one night, when the door slammed shut and he found himself trapped in total darkness.

"Haah, I finally caught you!" Mrs. Royson's voice was gleeful as she wedged the door shut.

Running in panic to the door, Apollo scratched at it wildly.

"Forget it mutt! This is the last night you'll be tormenting me and poor Lass."

CHAPTER 8

Apollo woke to long shafts of light filtering around the margins of the door and through cracks in the shiplap siding. He had spent much of the night pacing and digging at any little defect that suggested a potential avenue of escape from this prison. If there was a way out of this shed, he couldn't find it – he was truly trapped and at the mercy of Mrs. Royson.

As the day wore on, the interior of the little shed grew hotter and hotter. By midday, he was panting constantly, and whining with each breath he drew. He was worried. What was to become of him now? Would Mrs. Royson just leave him locked in here until he died of thirst?

Toward the middle of the afternoon, Apollo stopped panting, held his breath, and perked his one good ear in the direction of the door. What was that sound? There it was again – humans talking, and the sound of their voices was getting closer.

"It's taken me weeks, but I finally caught him!" Mrs. Royson pronounced proudly. "I could never get him to come to me, so I baited him into the shed. Last night while he was pigging out on the food I left for him, I was able to sneak over and slam the door shut on him."

"Is he aggressive?" a male voice asked. It was the policeman.

"I have no idea," Mrs. Royson replied. "I just know he's been a darned nuisance around here for the last month."

Apollo backed away from the door as it opened a crack. He shivered convulsively and slunk to the back of the shed as the policeman peeked in at him.

"Watch he doesn't get away!" Mrs. Royson cried as the policeman opened the door a bit wider.

"I don't think that's very likely," he responded. "The poor thing looks terrified."

The policeman entered the shed and took a step in Apollo's direction. Extending his hand, he took another step closer.

"Easy fella...there's a good boy," he said in a calm, quiet voice. "Do you want to come with me?"

Apollo quivered and shrunk back as the policeman advanced. Both ears lay flat to his head as the policeman slipped a noose over Apollo's head and around his neck.

"Come boy," he encouraged.

Apollo responded to a tug on the lead, and got to his feet on trembling legs.

"You can open it now," the policeman said as he approached the door.

Mrs. Royson was peering through a crack in the door but still leaning firmly against it. "Are you sure you have him?" Her voice sounded urgent.

"I'm sure," he said. "Come boy."

Apollo fell into step behind the policeman as the door swung open. The dog had been well-schooled by his owners on leash etiquette, and right now it seemed wise to follow orders.

"Finally." Mrs. Royson sighed with relief. "I'll be so glad to see an end to him."

The policeman stooped, stroked Apollo's still-trembling head and massaged his ears. "He's obviously been someone's pet along the way."

The policeman walked halfway across the yard with Apollo following obediently at his heel.

"Sit!" the policeman said forcefully.

Apollo slowed to a stop and sank to the ground.

"He listens better than my own dog," the policeman said.

"What are you going to do with him?" Mrs. Royson asked.

"It seems a shame, but I guess I'll have to take him to the dump and do away with him. I'd keep him myself if it wasn't for the fact that I already have a dog. Roland's a boxer and not good with other dogs. Big cities would have a pound for a dog like him, but small towns around here sure don't." The policeman knelt by Apollo who still cowered at his heel. "Are you thirsty boy?" He looked up at Mrs. Royson. "Can you get this poor dog a drink?"

Mrs. Royson walked to a standpipe near the house, filled a pink plastic bucket with water, and handed it to the policeman. The moment the policeman put it down in front of him, Apollo dove his head into the bucket and lapped voraciously at the water.

"Thought you looked a bit dry," the policeman said with a smile.

The policeman waited for Apollo to quit drinking before heading to his car. The moment he opened the back door of his vehicle,

Apollo jumped in and perched attentively on the seat. He had spent many happy hours with his former owners driving around the countryside, and just the thought of escaping the clutches of Mrs. Royson gave him hope of better things to come.

The policeman shook his head and smiled at Mrs. Royson. "He's certainly been in a vehicle before."

Apollo looked expectantly over the policeman's shoulder as they drove down the road toward the highway. Watching through the side window, Apollo saw the farm with the chicken yard come into view and pass behind them. He felt strangely at ease in this car – maybe the nice policeman was taking him home.

The policeman threw his hat on the seat beside him and peered into the rearview mirror. He shook his head in disbelief at his passenger. The dog sat comfortably on the seat, peering out the front window as if he had been his own pet for years.

That all changed when the policeman turned down a narrow tree-clad lane and came to a stop at the local dump. Apollo looked anxiously from side to side and twirled around on the seat. This place looked all too familiar. This was where he had gotten so terribly ill; this was where the big black creature had chased him; this was where humans came to discard things that were no longer of value to them.

Apollo whined and dropped his ears flat to his head as the policeman got out of the vehicle, opened the back door, and grabbed hold of the leash that now lay tangled on the seat.

"Come boy," he commanded.

Apollo dug his claws into the fabric of the seat and resisted as the policeman pulled on the lead. His ears lay flat to his head as smells of decay from this vile place filled his nostrils and the horrible memories of his past experiences made him panic. He whined and began trembling as the policeman pulled firmly on the leash. The policeman closed his eyes and pursed his lips as he looked at his charge.

"It's like you already know what's going to happen," he said.

With a concerted effort, the policeman dragged his prisoner from the backseat and out onto the recently upturned soil of the dumpsite. Perusing the contours of the refuse site, he looked for somewhere inconspicuous to dispose of the dog's body.

"Come boy," he said in a raspy voice. "Come on…it'll be all right."

The policeman stopped at the top of a bank next to a pile of discarded lumber. Apollo lay trembling on the ground, his ears flat to his head and his big brown eyes focused pleadingly on the policeman.

"I'm sorry boy," the policeman mumbled. Unsnapping the holster at his hip, he removed his pistol. "I just don't see what else I can do with you."

The policeman stood there with his pistol pointed at the dog's head. His hand trembled. Several times he closed his eyes and tightened his grip on the pistol, but each time he opened his eyes and saw the dog his finger backed away from the trigger. Finally, he shook his head in disgust and returned his pistol to its holster.

"Come on, you big boob, let's get out of here."

Apollo eagerly followed the policeman to the car and jumped up onto the backseat. He was filled with relief as the policeman turned his car around and headed back down the dirt road to the highway. Peering from one window to the next along the curvy roadway, Apollo watched hopefully for signs of home. On numerous occasions along the way, he thought that something looked vaguely familiar, but nothing really looked exactly right. After more than an hour of driving, they arrived in a town the dog had never seen before.

CHAPTER 9

The policeman pulled off the main drag and stopped in front of the squat brick building that served as the RCMP headquarters. He looked at the big dog peering at him from the backseat of his car and sighed. "How did I get myself into this mess?"

Taking a deep breath, the policeman got out of the patrol car. Opening the back door, he waited for Apollo to jump down to the sidewalk. The moment the policeman entered the building with Apollo in tow, he pronounced in a loud voice, "Anyone interested in a good German Shepherd dog?" He looked at the lady behind the counter. "How about it, Lynn?"

The pleasant blonde woman smiled at him through the safety glass that separated them. "Sorry, Ben, but the last thing I need right now is another dog."

Ben went into the back and looked at the burly corporal behind the desk. "How about it, Boomer? He's a real nice dog."

Boomer smiled as he looked at Apollo and shook his head knowingly. "Just couldn't do it, eh?"

Ben pursed his lips. "I'm such a sucker for critters." He looked at Boomer's grinning face. "So you don't know anyone who needs a dog?"

The big man just smiled at Ben and shook his head.

Apollo lay patiently on the floor while Ben sat at a desk and wrote on some papers. Shortly after, Ben left the station and loaded Apollo back into the patrol car. Apollo was anxious to see what Ben was going to do with him. Maybe he would take him home to his owners. Home – how he'd love to see his owners again! He would jump all over them and lick them half to death.

With a feeling of resignation, Ben started the engine and drove home. He brought the car to a stop in front of a comfortable-looking bungalow with a manicured lawn and a fenced backyard. Shutting off the engine, Ben sighed deeply and turned to look at Apollo. "What now?"

Apollo cocked his head at the sound of Ben's voice, then twirled excitedly around on the seat, certain that something exciting was about to happen. Opening the back door, Ben grabbed hold of the leash. "Come on fella, let's water your horse."

Ben led Apollo down the street, stopping at each power pole they passed, waiting for the dog to sniff out the ground and mark his territory. He continued the length of the street with Apollo at his heel, then returned to the home where the walk had begun.

Leading him through a gate at the side of the property, Ben tied the leash to a small ash tree. "You stay here while I go inside."

Apollo followed until the leash tightened, then sat to watch Ben disappear into the house. After a few moments, the door opened again and Ben returned with two little girls in tow.

"He's pretty daddy...can we keep him?" one girl chirped excitedly.

"I don't know sweetie. We'll see. You know Roland; he may never want to share you with another dog. Besides that, I'm not sure if this guy will be good with children. We don't want to take any chances with you and your sister."

As the humans approached, Apollo stood up and slowly wagged his tail.

"See daddy, he likes us," the girl asserted. "Maybe Roland will like him too."

"We'll see sweetie…we'll see."

Ben left his children a few steps behind him while he slipped a bowl of food in front of Apollo. Apollo dove into the crunchies with a passion, all the while keeping an eye on the humans as they stood back to watch him eat.

Apollo spent the night on the back porch away from the rest of the household. Several times during the early evening he exchanged growls back and forth through the door that separated him from the family within. Each time he responded, angry barking erupted, until the outbreak was brought up short by Ben as he scolded Roland.

Early the next morning, the door opened a crack and Ben squeezed through, making an effort to prevent Roland from following him. Putting Apollo back on his leash, he wandered about with him in the backyard until the dog had done his duties. They were heading toward the back porch when the door suddenly swung open.

"Nicole, no!" Ben hollered. "Don't let him out!"

It was too late – the muscular boxer flew through the opening and charged straight at Apollo. The two dogs rolled end over end with teeth gnashing. The early morning silence was punctured by the growling of two dogs, the yelling of a man, and the tearful wailing of a child.

By the time Ben had separated the dogs and dragged Roland back into the house, he was beside himself. "This just isn't going to work!" he hollered. Slamming the back door to separate the two combatants, Ben settled Nicole down, and picked up the phone.

It took Apollo a while to settle down after his battle with Roland. This had been the first real encounter with another dog where he had had to fight to defend himself, and it had left his heart racing. His neck was painful from where Roland had grabbed him, and he was bleeding from several spots on his front paws.

Apollo was licking his right front paw when Ben came out of the house and picked up the leash still dangling from the dog's collar. "Come boy…let's get this over with."

Apollo could see that Ben's attitude toward him had changed — there was a feeling of tension in the air as the policeman took the dog to the car and opened the back door.

The moment Apollo hopped in, Ben got in the car and started driving. After a few minutes, he pulled up in front of a tall white building. Apollo watched intently as Ben opened the front door and stepped inside. The dog was wondering what was about to happen, because the policeman had definitely not been happy with him after the big fight in his backyard.

Within a few minutes, Ben reappeared with a tall, lanky man. This man got Apollo's attention immediately. Although he was young and dressed in blue jeans similar to those his former owner had worn, the man was also draped in a white wrap-around smock that immediately invoked in Apollo scary memories of when his former owners had brought him to a hospital for surgery on his ear. The people who had worked in that place and done painful things to him had all worn uniforms just like that.

Ben's face was flushed and his eyes downcast as he opened the door of the car and tried to coax the dog out. Suspecting something was amiss, Apollo remained perched nervously on the edge of the seat with his claws dug into the fabric. Only when Ben gave a very vigorous tug on the leash did Apollo lower his front paws to the curb.

"I hate to ask you to put him away, Dave," Ben said to the man, "but I just can't bring myself to do it. I've never wanted anything to do with being an animal control officer, but in rural areas like this it's supposedly part of our duties. I could never have been a veterinarian either…I'm just too softhearted."

Dr. Dave nodded. "I know how you feel. I hate putting animals down unless they're suffering. Even then I ask myself why I should have the right to play God."

"Well, better you than me," Ben said. "I find it hard enough to bring Roland in for his shots. The two times I've picked up owner-less dogs that had been hit by cars and brought them in to you, I couldn't get out of here fast enough. I don't know how you can stand it."

"There are often pretty tough choices to be made," Dr. Dave responded. "Still new at this myself…haven't even been in Creston for a year yet."

"I had this big goof at the Crawford Bay dump with the intention of doing away with him," Ben said. "I aimed at his head a half dozen times, and each time he looked at me with the saddest eyes… Like he knew what was coming. I just couldn't pull the trigger."

"So what's the problem with him? Has he been aggressive and bitten someone?"

"No, nothing like that…It's kind of a long story. This mutt's a stray who has caused us no end of misery at the office. He's been running loose down at Crawford Bay, killing chickens, and tormenting a woman and her dog. We got so many complaints about him, we eventually had to do something. When the woman finally trapped him in her woodshed, I was elected to be his executioner." Ben paused for a moment, and then continued. "It's a crying shame to have to destroy a dog like him."

Dr. Dave chuckled. "Why don't you bring him in where I can have a better look at him."

Apollo suspiciously followed Ben along the street until he approached the doorway of the building. But the moment Apollo crossed the threshold, he panicked. He planted all four paws and struggled to get back outside. Bracing himself, Ben dragged Apollo inside and Dr. Dave closed the door behind him.

"He's obviously been to a veterinary facility before," Dr. Dave observed. "He picked up on the smell of the place right away."

"I feel like such a jerk condemning this poor thing to death," Ben said. "I brought him to my place with the hope of finding a home for him, but he and my own dog got into it right away. If I hadn't been there to break them up this morning, you'd have had some work to do putting one or both of them back together again. I've got two little girls at home and just can't have this sort of thing going on."

Ben stroked Apollo's head as the dog lay quivering at his feet. "It looks as if he's been through the mill in the last little while, but I couldn't see anything seriously wrong with him."

Dr. Dave knelt a few feet from Apollo and extended his open hand. "Come over here fella," he coaxed in a soothing tone. "Come on you big lug...I'm not going to hurt you."

As terrified as Apollo was, he wanted desperately to trust someone.

"There's a boy," Dr. Dave continued. "You really are a nice fellow aren't you?"

Raising his head just inches from the floor and keeping his belly flat to the ground, Apollo crawled over and stuck his muzzle in Dr. Dave's hand.

"There we go." Dr. Dave continued to stroke Apollo and rumple his ears. "You really are a fine looking specimen aren't you?"

It had been a long time since anyone had talked like this to Apollo, and not once since he had run off from his owners had anyone stroked him so gently. The dog had forgotten just how much he craved his owners' attention.

Dr. Dave stood and took a few steps back to sit on a waiting room bench. He patted his leg. "Come boy...come over here."

Apollo stared at him for a few seconds before slowly rising to a standing position and creeping ever so slowly in Dr. Dave's direction. At first, Apollo only extended his muzzle, but within a few minutes he was leaning against the vet's leg and extending his head to Dr. Dave's lap in search of more petting.

"Well, it sure looks like he's warming up to you," Ben observed.

"It's taken me more than a day to get to the point where he lets me touch him without cringing."

Dr. Dave stood, removed Apollo's leash and returned it to Ben. "By the look of things, you can stop feeling guilty about condemning this dog to death. We'll keep him here to see if we can find a good home for him. I'd have as much trouble as you doing away with him."

CHAPTER 10

"You've taken in another one, have you, Dave?"

Apollo looked apprehensively at Doris, the vet's receptionist, as she entered the waiting room. He was uneasy…After living alone for all those weeks, and working hard to avoid contact with people, this sudden introduction of so many new faces was hard to handle. Apollo had just gotten to the point of halfway trusting the policeman, and now he found himself with his head in the lap of Dr. Dave.

"Come say hi to this big lug in case you have to handle him in the back, and take him out of the kennel." Dr. Dave sensed Apollo's discomfort as Doris approached, and kept his palm over the dog's muzzle. The vet was still uncertain as to how the dog would react to yet another stranger. Apollo trembled as Doris laid her hands on his forehead and gave him a gentle pat.

"Looks like he's been through some rough times," she said, noticing the caked blood on Apollo's ear from the fight earlier in the day. "It's okay boy, I'm not going to hurt you." Doris ran her hand down the nape of the dog's neck.

Dr. Dave smiled at Doris. "How about you grab a choke chain

and leash and we'll take him into the exam room and give him a quick going over."

When Doris returned with the chain and leash, Dr. Dave slipped it over Apollo's head, stood up, and proceeded to the exam room with his patient at his heel. Apollo tensed as the vet stooped, wrapped one arm around the dog's neck, the other around his butt, and hefted him onto the stainless steel table. Apollo's eyes widened and filled with terror at this unexpected turn of events; his body trembled so badly he shook the entire table.

"You're just fine fella," Dr. Dave asserted, stroking Apollo's head. "We're not going to hurt you. We just want to check you out and make sure there's nothing wrong with you."

Doris stepped in next to the table and took the dog's head in her hands. "Oh, he's so worried." She continued stroking Apollo until he relaxed a bit, then slowly wrapped her arm around his neck, corralling his head against her bosom. Apollo tensed again as Dr. Dave ran his hands over both sides of his body, then checked each leg, one after the other. He squirmed when the vet lifted his tail and stuck something cold in his bum.

Dr. Dave bent close to focus on a wound to the pad of Apollo's right front paw, then moved on to examine the small rent in his ear. Then the vet left the room, leaving Apollo alone with Doris. He looked up at her with apprehension in his eyes as she relaxed her grip and gently stroked his head. "You're okay boy," she assured him, "you're in good hands now."

Dr. Dave returned with a bowl of warm water that he set on the table. Doris's grip on Apollo tightened as the vet gently picked up the sore paw, poured some brown stuff on it, and began scrubbing.

"Sometimes I wonder about you, Dave," Doris said ruefully. "We just found homes for two strays last week and now you're taking up another kennel with this big brute. It makes it hard for me to book surgeries when I'm not even sure we have room at the inn."

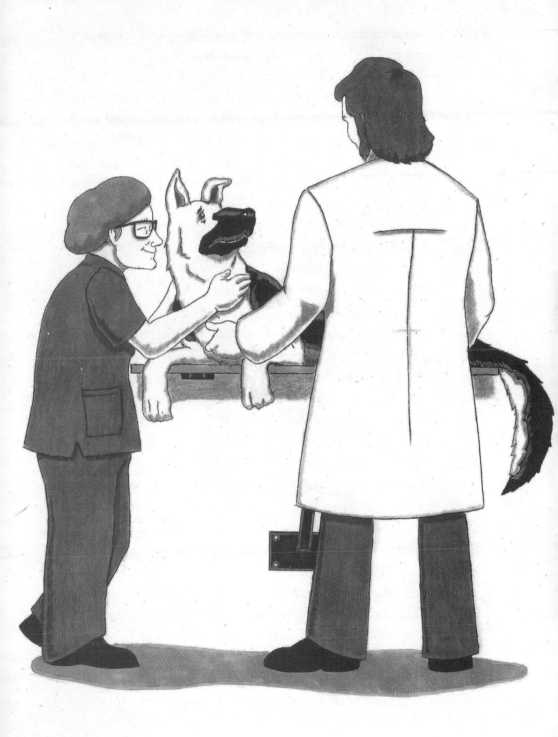

"What would you have me do: Put him down, and dump him in the freezer?" Dr. Dave replied sarcastically.

"No," Doris sighed, "he's too nice a dog for that."

Apollo relaxed as Dr. Dave worked on his paw and gently shaved some hair from the top of his foot. He squirmed and worried more when the vet scrubbed at his ear and started shaving it. He didn't want anyone fooling with that ear again – he had had enough of that.

Dr. Dave wrinkled his brow and absently shook his head. "Someone's probably missing this dog. I'm pretty sure he's a purebred Shepherd, and his former owner must have spent some pretty major coin to get this ear fixed up."

"What's been done to it?" Doris asked.

"He's had what's called a lateral ear ablation where the entire ear canal has been surgically removed. It's only done when there's been a chronic unresponsive infection or a very serious injury… That's why the ear looks kind of floppy."

Dr. Dave finished scrubbing the ear, then took the thermometer out of Apollo's rectum. He wiped the thermometer clean with paper towel, held it up to the light to read it, and stuck it back in a container of disinfectant.

Apollo was straining against Doris's grasp to turn his head and figure out what Dr. Dave was up to, when the vet stuck a stethoscope in his ears and moved the head of the apparatus around on Apollo's side. It didn't hurt, but the dog wanted to know what was going on.

Suddenly, Apollo heard the opening and closing of the office door and then the apprehensive panting and whining of another dog.

"We'll be right with you!" Doris hollered. "Our first appointment is here," she said quietly to her boss. "And this one's a paying customer."

The vet smiled at his receptionist. "This guy's pretty thin," he continued, as if unaware of the interruption, "but his temperature's normal, and those wounds look superficial…Can't see anything that a few days of cage rest and some good grub won't fix."

Doris released her grip on Apollo as Dr. Dave hefted him back onto the floor. Before he knew what was going on, the dog was being led through the front office to another part of the building. He looked askance at a gray-haired man cuddling an old poodle in the waiting room and nervously followed Dr. Dave through a door into a small room with lots of strange smells. Apollo put on the brakes and tried to retreat, but before he could head back, Dr. Dave closed the door behind them.

Apollo nervously took a few steps into the room and looked around. Against one wall were kennels similar to the one he had once been housed in when they had done something to his ear. He tensed as a dog barked in one of the kennels and a cat in one of the upper kennels meowed and stuck its paw through the bars for attention.

"It's okay fella," Dr. Dave assured him. "You won't be here for long. A good-looking dog like you…we'll have no trouble finding you a home."

The moment Dr. Dave released his grip on the leash, Apollo headed to the door to sniff under it, hoping for some way out of this place. But when he saw no hope of going back, he gave up and wandered around the crowded little room, dragging the leash behind him. He sniffed briefly at the washer, drier and refrigerator, then checked out a couple of bins that smelled like food.

"You hungry fella?" Dr. Dave asked. "Don't worry, we'll start putting some meat on those big bones of yours."

Apollo looked up at the upper level in this storage bin for animals. One cat persistently stuck out its paw for attention, while another in the middle cage was hardly visible as it hid behind its litter box. At the far end, a little white poodle looked mournfully down on Apollo. Half asleep, the poodle could care less what was going on around it. A bigger dog in a bottom kennel only had one eye and had something hanging on the cage door in front of it.

Dr. Dave grabbed a thick woollen blanket from a shelf, then knelt to open one of the bigger kennel doors on the bottom tier. Spreading the blanket out on the floor of the enclosure, he took great care at smoothing it out. Picking up a metal bowl, he wandered to one of the bins and scooped up some dry dog food.

Apollo's eyes brightened when Dr. Dave opened the fridge, took out a can, and scooped a couple of dollops of nice red meat into the bowl. He remembered when Jim would bring cans of food like that home to spoil him once in a while.

He was extending his head to the bowl, which rested in the center of the room, when Dr. Dave grabbed hold of his leash and led him to the entrance of the kennel. Apollo struggled as Dr. Dave unsnapped the leash and forced him head first into the kennel. Slamming the door behind him, the vet trapped the dog in the tiny space.

"You're all right, you big boob," Dr. Dave reassured.

Apollo whined mournfully as he peered through the metal bars. All the bad memories of his being trapped in one of these horrible cages came flooding back. Apollo heard the door to the room open and close as Dr. Dave left to see his next patient. He shifted his long legs in the confined space, trying to get comfortable. But it was no use. How could a big dog like him get comfortable in a tiny space like this?

Apollo listened intently to try and figure out what was going on in this strange place. He could hear the muffled sounds of humans talking as he lay there looking out at the appliances on the other side of the room. Occasionally he could hear the screeching of tires on the street outside and the rattling of big trucks as they drove over a pothole in front of the clinic.

Half an hour after being locked up, Apollo heard the door to the kennel room open. Dr. Dave extended a few fingers between the bars and Apollo sniffed at them. He watched as the vet grabbed another bowl from a shelf and left the room. A few minutes later, Dr. Dave returned with the bowl filled with water. He knelt in front of Apollo's enclosure and opened the door to the kennel.

The moment he saw the open door, Apollo struggled to stand and escape. Dr. Dave gently but forcefully put his hand on the dog's back. "Not now fella."

Dr. Dave placed the bowl of water in the cage, then grabbed the food dish from the center of the room and placed it inside as well. Closing the door, he stood back to observe his reluctant guest.

Apollo peered out at him, and Dr. Dave opened the door once more, grabbed a chunk of the canned dog food and put it right under Apollo's nose. At first Apollo just turned away as if he wasn't interested in the offering, but as the vet stroked his head with one hand and kept the food in front of him with the other, the dog relented.

After Apollo had eaten the first few bites, Dr. Dave put the food bowl in front of him and watched with satisfaction as the dog continued eating.

"There's a fellow," the vet told him. "You'll look way better with a few extra pounds on that frame of yours."

Apollo kept eating until the dish was empty. He had just finished polishing off the last kernels of food when a teenage boy came into the room. Opening the kennel above Apollo, the boy removed a blanket and threw it into the washing machine. Apollo heard the boy squirting something from a bottle and could smell the strong scent of disinfectant. When the boy had finished what he was doing with that cage, he went on to the next. Dumping the contents of a cat litter box into the garbage, he went to the fridge, took out a small can and scooped something into a dish. "Good kittie," the boy said as he put the dish into the cage.

Apollo watched apprehensively as the boy hefted the poodle down from the top kennel, slipped a choke chain over his head and disappeared out the back door with him. He was gone for awhile before he came crashing back in, banging the rickety old doors behind him. He lifted the poodle back up into its kennel then stopped in front of Apollo.

"Hello there big fella," the boy said, sticking a few fingers through he bars.

Apollo retreated to the very back of the kennel as the boy undid the latch to the door. Emitting a low rumble from deep in his throat, Apollo glared at the boy as he started to open the door. The boy flushed, closed the door, replaced the latch, and backed away. He disappeared and returned with Dr. Dave.

"I'm sorry to bother you, Dr. Perrin, but you told me to ask for help if I was afraid of any of your patients."

"Not a problem, Danny…Better to be safe than sorry."

"I don't think he likes me," Danny said uncertainly. "He

growled at me and I didn't want to take any chances."

Dr. Dave knelt before the cage and opened the door. "I think this poor guy's just a little overwhelmed with everything that's been going on."

Apollo licked his lips and wagged the very tip of his tail as Dr. Dave extended his hand to him. "Come on, you big lug. It's time for your walk."

Apollo relaxed as Dr. Dave gently stroked the top of his head. The very mention of that four letter word – 'walk' – had certainly peeked his interest. The moment the vet grabbed the end of the choke chain and said, "Come," Apollo bolted out onto the kennel room floor.

"Just give me the leash," Dr. Dave said to Danny.

After snapping the leash onto the eye of the chain, Dr. Dave handed the leash to Danny. Still kneeling beside Apollo, Dr. Dave gave him a few pats then ruffled his ears. "This is Danny, and he's going to be taking you for long walks over the next few days." He turned to Danny. "Give this guy an extra long walk and stop several times just to pet him. Give him a couple of treats along the way and make sure that you're the one to put him back into his kennel." He grabbed a few milk bones from a bag on the counter and handed them to Danny. "Leave him a big scoop of canned dog food and you won't have any trouble with him tomorrow morning."

Apollo was nervous as Danny half dragged him through a rickety old door and down a narrow, dark passage way. He waited while the boy opened yet another door that opened into a back room stacked with boxes. He stood nervously wondering what would happen next, when the boy opened the outside door and Apollo charged out into the daylight. The leash snapped tight as Danny struggled to pull the door closed. With Apollo leading the way, they charged off toward the back alley.

By the time Apollo was halfway down the block, he was

beginning to settle down. Danny stopped and hesitantly reached out to pet him. When Apollo seemed to appreciate it, the boy slipped a milk bone from his pocket and held it out where Apollo could take it. After wolfing it down, he nudged the boy's hand for another. By the time they arrived back at the clinic, Danny and Apollo were comfortable with one another, and although Apollo hated going back into the kennel, he did as he was told.

CHAPTER 11

The next days were tough on Apollo as he learned to get used to being kennelled for most of the day. The food was good and he loved it when Danny showed up to take him for his walks. Often, late in the evenings, Dr. Dave would take him outside too.

Apollo wished he could spend more time with Dr. Dave, but the vet was always so busy with the other animals. Apollo was growing very fond of Dr. Dave and his gentle way of handling him. The dog knew the vet lived somewhere above him in the same building, because every night Dr. Dave would come down and check on all of his patients. And he never missed an opportunity to open Apollo's door and have a chat with him.

Apollo was asleep one evening when the door to the kennel room opened and the light clicked on. Dr. Dave wandered from kennel to kennel checking on his patients one at a time as he always did. When he got to Apollo's kennel he just opened the door and walked away. Apollo lay there for a moment staring at the open door and wondering what he was supposed to do. As no one was telling him otherwise, he got up and stepped down onto the floor. After a quick look around the kennel room, Apollo wandered out into the surgery. He walked the perimeter of the room, sniffing here and there, taking in all the weird, unusual smells that the veterinary clinic had to offer. After a minute of snooping, Apollo headed to the waiting room where Dr. Dave sat on the waiting room bench writing on his cards.

For a moment, Apollo just stood staring at the vet as he focused on his work, paying absolutely no heed to the dog. After a bit, Apollo wandered over and sat next to Dr. Dave. When the vet still made no offer to pay attention to him, Apollo nudged his hand.

"Hey there, you big lug, are you lonely?" Dr. Dave asked. Putting aside his paperwork, he stroked Apollo's head and gently checked the scabbed bite wound at the tip of his ear. After a minute of petting, Apollo lifted his front paws onto the waiting room bench and rested his head on the vet's lap. When Dr. Dave started writing on his cards again, Apollo lifted first one hind leg then the other up onto the bench. The whole time he focused his gaze on Dr. Dave's face for any sign of disapproval. This was when Barb would have said, "Apollo, no!" But as Dr. Dave said nothing, Apollo stretched out on his side and rested his head on the vet's lap.

When Dr. Dave finally finished writing and got up, Apollo stared at him sleepily.

"Ready for a walk?"

Apollo was on his feet and on the floor in a second. By the time Dr. Dave returned with a leash, the dog was dancing in circles and vocalizing his excitement.

They wandered down the street past the mill yard, and then back up the main street. When they returned to the clinic, Dr. Dave unhooked the leash and went to the kennel room. Pointing to Apollo's cage, he gruffly told him one word, "Kennel." How Apollo was growing to hate that word!

Apollo crawled in and curled up. The lights went out, and he listened to the sound of Dr. Dave climbing the stairs and walking across the creaky floor overhead to his bedroom.

The following day, late in the morning, Doris came to see Apollo. Grabbing a leash from the hook on the wall, she knelt before his kennel and opened the door. Apollo wagged his tail vigorously as she connected the leash to his choke chain. He was excited – now even Doris was going to take him for a walk!

When Apollo skidded around the corner toward the front door, he stopped short. A stocky young man he had never seen before was standing in the middle of the waiting room staring at him. The moment he saw him, Apollo backed up behind Doris and emitted a low rumble from his throat. There was something he just didn't like about this guy.

"He's still shy around strangers," Doris said defensively.

"That's okay," the man answered, "I like aggressive dogs."

Just at that moment, Dr. Dave came trudging through the office door with gum boots dangling from his hand and a pair of dirty coveralls rolled up and tucked under his armpit. The moment he was through the door, Apollo rushed over to him and nuzzled his free hand, dragging Doris along with him.

"This gentleman is interested in our stray," Doris said pleasantly.

Stepping forward, the man took the leash from Doris. "He's a bit skittish," he said dubiously, "but I'll take him."

Apollo panicked as the man tried to drag him closer. Giving Dr. Dave a terrified look, Apollo struggled to get back to him.

Dr. Dave set his boots on the floor, his coveralls on the waiting room bench, and took the leash from the man. Apollo rushed instantly to Dr. Dave and cowered behind his legs.

"I'm sorry Doris, didn't you see the note I left on his card?"

Doris looked confused. "Note? What note is that?"

Dr. Dave grabbed his boots from the floor and headed to the kennel room with Apollo at his heel, leaving Doris and the man standing in the waiting room.

"What was all that about?" Doris asked after the man had left.

She authoritatively waved a patient record card in front of Dr. Dave's face. "There's not a darn thing written on here!"

Apollo was still hanging close to Dr. Dave.

"Did you like that guy, Doris?"

"What do you mean?"

"Just what I asked…Did he look like the type of guy you would like to have your daughter dating?"

"Well, no, but what has that got to do with giving a dog away?"

"Less than a month ago I saw that guy driving around town with a big dog hanging out of the back of his truck. God knows what happened to that one."

Doris sighed as Dr. Dave went on.

"You didn't like him, I didn't like him, and the dog sure as heck didn't like him, and that explains the note on the card!"

Dr. Dave smiled at his befuddled receptionist and headed into the back room. "I'm going upstairs to make some lunch."

"What are you going to do with the stray?" she asked as Apollo followed along behind Dr. Dave.

"He can't hurt much up here," he hollered as he walked up the stairs. "He can share some of my moldy bread."

Apollo was ecstatic as he plodded up the stairs behind Dr. Dave. He was finally feeling like he belonged somewhere. As he followed Dr. Dave to the refrigerator, and from there to the table, Apollo thought that just maybe he could make something work out with Dr. Dave. Plunking himself down beside the table, he watched as Dr. Dave buttered his bread. He stood up and licked his lips as the vet opened a package of salami and flipped a couple of slabs onto his creation. The moment the vet sat down, Apollo positioned himself at his elbow waiting for a handout. Dr. Dave had already eaten half of his sandwich when Apollo reached up with his nose and gently nudged his elbow.

"You think you need some, do you?" Dr. Dave smiled and

ripped the remainder of his sandwich in half. "Just don't think we're going to make a habit of this."

It was a real letdown for Apollo when, after lunch, Dr. Dave marched him to his kennel and locked him back in. He watched as the vet pulled on his coveralls and slipped on some boots. He had come to recognize that Dr. Dave's coveralls always smelled so much more interesting when he marched back into this room than they did when he went out. Apollo so wanted to go with him to see what exciting things he got up to outside.

The kennel room was a beehive of activity throughout the day. Early in the day almost every other animal that had been one of Apollo's kennelmates had been discharged. After Dr. Dave returned from his outside venture and threw a very whiffy pair of coveralls into the clothes basket, there had been a constant flow of new patients coming in. The kennel above was now occupied by a cat that had something hooked to it, and a dog in the kennel next to Apollo had been carried in a few minutes earlier and he was hooked to something too. That dog was whining and yelping constantly, and Apollo was elated when Danny arrived to take him for a walk. That constant racket was getting on his nerves.

Danny and Apollo were just passing through the office when Dr. Dave called out, "Danny, before you go out with the stray, clean out his kennel and get it ready for this guy…We're running short of kennels."

Dr. Dave had a dog on the same table that Apollo had been on, and this patient didn't look so good. She appeared much like Lass must have looked in her younger years, but in her present state she could hardly hold her head up. Dr. Dave had something hanging from a pole over her, and it looked as if she was hooked up to it too.

Danny pointed to Apollo. "What are we going to do with this guy?"

"I guess for now we'll stick him in the surgery kennel," Dr. Dave replied.

As Danny took the blankets and food dishes from Apollo's kennel and sprayed down the inside walls with the smelly stuff, Apollo lay on the waiting room floor and took in all of the activity around him.

"Did you call all the other clinics about the stray?" Dr. Dave asked Doris as he worked on the patient he had on the table.

"I called Trail, Nelson, Cranbrook, and Fernie, and none of them could think of a German Shepherd patient that had a lateral ear ablation…and none of them have had a report of a German Shepherd being missing in their area."

"That's too bad. I was almost sure someone would have been looking for him."

The telephone rang and Doris rushed to the front desk to answer it. She listened for a moment before responding in a sympathetic tone, "Oh Mrs. Ross, I'm so sorry to hear that. Sebastian was such a sweetheart." She listened for a moment more then looked right at Apollo when she answered. "We do have…He's a big beautiful German Shepherd. We've had him here for over a week now and he's become a real favorite around here." She paused and listened for a few moments more. "Okay, we can do that. We'll see you next Friday." Doris looked right at Apollo when she made her pronouncement. Then she rushed back to help Dr. Dave in the exam room.

"That was Mrs. Ross from down the lake," she continued. "You remember Sebastian, the big half German Shepherd half Saint Bernard that we neutered last month? Well, he got hit on the highway and killed last week and Mrs. Ross says she's absolutely lost without a dog around the place. She can't come in to town till the end of the week, but she asked us to keep this guy until she gets here. She says she'll pay for his board until she's able to pick him up."

"That would certainly be a good home for the big lout," Dr. Dave admitted grudgingly.

"You sure don't sound very enthused about it," Doris noted. "Are you sure you want to let him go? You seem to be getting rather attached to him."

Dr. Dave looked rather longingly at Apollo. "Of course we'll let him go. How could I possibly keep a big dog like him around here?"

Doris gave Dr. Dave a knowing look. "Are you sure you don't want me to call Mrs. Ross and tell her this dog's already taken?"

"No, of course not. He's just a big nuisance around here, and he's taking up kennel space that we can use for other animals. We're full to the brim tonight, and if another animal comes in, I don't have a clue what we'll do with him."

When Danny finished cleaning the kennel and grabbed the leash to walk Apollo, Dr. Dave cut him off. "Danny, can you put the partition under the surgery table and get the kennel ready for this big lug and the guy on the table? I'm finished here for now, so I'll take him for a walk."

Apollo pulled happily on the lead as they made their way down the alley. Lifting his leg at all the strategic poles and on the more prominent corners of the buildings, he stopped here and there. Occasionally he would stick his nose into a clump of grass and give a few decisive snorts before going on to check out other spots that tantalized his olfactory senses.

They were at the end of the alley when Dr. Dave bent down and took off Apollo's lead to allow him to range freely on his own. Dr. Dave watched with his heart in his mouth as Apollo ran off ahead of him.

"Hey, you big lug, come back here!" he yelled.

As though stung by a bee, Apollo whipped around and came running back to him. Shoving his muzzle under Dr. Dave's hand, Apollo flipped his head a number of times to make sure the man's hand was in petting position. Apollo moaned as Dr. Dave rubbed his forehead and massaged his ears. Satisfied that he was in Dr. Dave's good books, he trotted ahead to check out the rest of the neighborhood.

They were on their way back to the clinic when Doris came running down the alley.

"Mel Griffith just came in the door, Dave," she blurted between puffs. "He ran over his old Lab and it looks like the dog might have a broken leg."

"Come here, you big lug," Dr. Dave hollered. "Your outing's over for the time being." Dr. Dave snapped the leash onto Apollo's collar and headed after Doris.

"You're getting pretty trusting," Doris said. "Aren't you worried about letting him off the leash?"

"He seems to stay close," Dr. Dave replied. "Besides, it's not as if he belongs to anyone. No one would miss him if he took off."

"Are you sure about that?" Doris muttered over her shoulder. "Looks to me like you might be a bit upset if he left."

Dr. Dave just grunted in reply.

Back at the clinic, Dr. Dave loaded Apollo into the surgery kennel that Danny had prepared and then went outside with Mel to help him carry in the new patient. They put the old Lab on top of the surgery table, right over where Apollo was housed. Apollo looked up at Dr. Dave with interest as he shifted around to examine the old dog.

"Sorry to keep you here after hours like this, Doc," Mel said. "I'd just stacked a load of empty boxes onto my trailer and was hauling them down to the shed for storage. I didn't realize that old Gabe had laid down in front of the wheel. I never thought to check for him when I took off, and I ran right over him with the trailer! He can't hear worth a darn any more, and his reactions aren't what they used to be, so I guess he never even woke up until the tire went over him."

Apollo lay with his head on his paws as Dr. Dave continued to work on the old dog. It was hours later when Dr. Dave knelt in front of Apollo's kennel and opened the door.

Giving the dog a big pat, he asked, "What're we going to do with you, ya big boob?"

Apollo sprang to his feet, wagging his tail in expectation.

"There's no place left for spongers around here," Dr. Dave told him.

Apollo stood back in his kennel surveying Dr. Dave's face for signs of approval.

"Okay, come on out," Dr. Dave encouraged. "It's all right."

Wagging his tail, Apollo danced around Dr. Dave hoping for another walk.

"Come on big fella," Dr. Dave told him. Apollo followed Dr. Dave as he rushed through the clinic and into the stairwell to the upstairs apartment. The dog was already climbing the stairs, excited

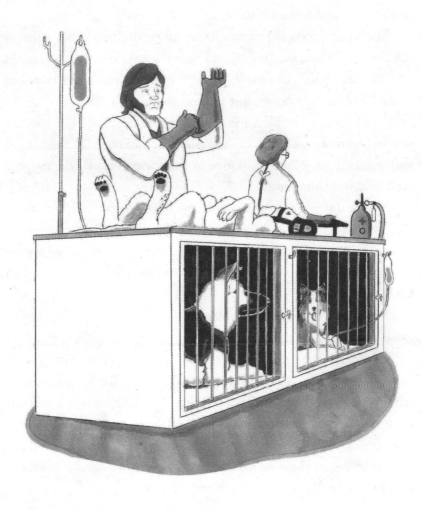

at the possibility that he would be up there with Dr. Dave, when the door closed behind him.

He could hear Dr. Dave's voice fading into the distance. "You just wait here until I figure out what to do with you."

Apollo walked to the top of the stairs and listened intently for sounds of what was going on in the clinic. At first he could hear three voices, then only Dr. Dave's and Doris's.

It was a while later, and he had almost gone to sleep, when he heard Dr. Dave's voice at the bottom of the stairwell. "Okay mutt, you can come down with us now."

Apollo hesitated at first, then ran down the stairs and through the clinic to stand wagging his tail at the front door.

"Not yet fella," Dr. Dave said. "We've still got some cleaning up to do before we can go out for another walk."

Apollo followed them into the surgery. He sniffed at the old yellow Lab that was asleep in the kennel he had been in, then stood and watched Dr. Dave and Doris as they wiped down the surgery table and put things away.

"What are you going to do with him tonight?" Doris asked. "Do you think he would bother any of the hospitalized patients?"

"I'm not sure," Dr. Dave admitted. "Ben said he was aggressive with other dogs, but I haven't seen any evidence of that since he's been here."

It was almost dark when Doris went home and Apollo and Dr. Dave were left alone. They went upstairs and Dr. Dave clicked on the TV before stretching out on the living room floor with a huge cushion propped under his chest. Apollo lay beside him, cuddling as close to the tall man as he could get. Dr. Dave often went down to the clinic to check on his patients, and each trip down and back up the stairs, Apollo was him, trotting at his heel. Apollo loved the feeling of being close to someone again and watched everything that Dr. Dave did with great interest.

Apollo was surprised that when it was time for their walk Dr. Dave just opened the clinic door and let him out without a leash. It was late at night, and the streets of the quiet little town were completely empty. Dr. Dave let Apollo walk ahead, but the dog constantly turned to make sure that his new would-be master was keeping up with him. They were walking past the mill yard when Apollo ran amongst the stacks of logs and came out with a stick in his mouth.

"Oh you like to play fetch, do you?" Dr. Dave asked as Apollo dropped the crooked stick at his feet. Apollo waited until Dr. Dave was about to pick it up, then grabbed it and ran off ahead. Tossing the stick high into the air, he caught it before it could hit the ground.

The next time he brought his trophy to Dr. Dave, Apollo dropped it at his feet and waited with anticipation until the vet picked it up and threw it.

By the time they returned to the clinic, Apollo was as happy as a dog could be. He walked from kennel to kennel with Dr. Dave as he checked on each of the patients and made sure that the hanging things kept dripping away. Both of Apollo's former kennels were occupied and he wondered where he would sleep tonight.

Later on, Dr. Dave fell asleep in front of the TV with Apollo's head on his lap. It was late when Dr. Dave got up, clicked off the TV, and made a final trip downstairs to make his rounds. He looked tired when he dragged himself back up to his apartment, and he headed straight to bed, leaving Apollo to choose where he would sleep. Wanting to be close to Dr. Dave, Apollo stretched out right next to the bed.

In the middle of the night, Apollo heard a crash downstairs. Getting to his feet, he turned to check on Dr. Dave, who was sound asleep and obviously not bothered by the noise. Apollo was about to lay back down when he heard another thud, like when Danny crashed open those rickety old doors to the back room. Maybe it was Danny.

Apollo walked through the apartment to the head of the stairs. All the doors were open, so he crept down the stairs and through the lab. Everything was quiet when he wandered through the office and out into the waiting room. Light shone in from the street lamps outside, and he could see nothing out of the ordinary. He was heading into the surgery when he saw something move.

For a moment he was scared – things didn't feel right. He stopped in his tracks and focused into the gloom of the other room. Suddenly a bright light clicked on and shone right in his eyes. Someone was here, and it wasn't Danny!

Apollo's heart began to race and the hair stood up on the back of his neck. He growled as the light continued to shine straight into his eyes. Whoever it was suddenly ran from the surgery and out through the doors at the back of the kennel room. Apollo barked fiercely and raced after the figure. All of the troubles that humans had heaped upon him were on his mind as he ran through the open doors in pursuit of the intruder who was now disappearing down the main street of town.

Apollo was just heading back to the open door when a car with a flashing red light screeched around the corner and came to a stop beside the clinic. A man hopped out and another bright light shone in Apollo's eyes. He barked ferociously and ran at the man, before slowly retreating to the open door.

"It's okay now boy...it's okay," said the man with the light.

Apollo would have nothing of it and kept barking furiously.

Dr. Dave came stumbling through the narrow passageway in a disheveled state. His feet were bare, his shirt was undone, and he was only just zipping up the fly on his blue jeans. "Here...settle down now, you big lug!" he hollered.

Apollo was so intent on protecting his newfound home that he hardly heard him.

"Easy now...easy now," Dr. Dave continued. "What's going on here?"

Apollo turned and wagged his tail at the sight of Dr. Dave. The dog's hair, which had been standing on end, slicked down under the flow of the vet's hand. Apollo worked his nose under Dr. Dave's hand and gave a couple of flips in search of support.

"Thank God you're here!" came a voice from out on the street.

"What in the world's going on?" Dr. Dave asked.

"My Lord, that dog just about tore the pants off me."

"Oh, it's you Ben," Dr. Dave said as he recognized the policeman.

As if his job was now done, Apollo took a few strides down the hall and lay down. Ben walked cautiously to the door and peered round the corner. The policeman had obviously developed a healthy respect for Apollo.

"I was driving down Canyon Street," Ben said breathlessly, "when I saw a guy running from this side of the street. He looked like he was in a real rush and I had a hunch that something wasn't right. I pulled over and had a look and that's when I noticed your back door was open."

Dr. Dave looked at the shards of splintered wood that still clung to the casing of the door frame. "Looks like it's been kicked in."

"I saw that," Ben said, "but when I tried to check it out, I saw why that other guy left in such a hurry. That dog just about took my leg off!"

Dr. Dave's face broke into a broad smile. "Talk about a lucky break – this is his first night on duty."

"That was awful good timing on your part," Ben said. "When did you decide to keep him as a watch dog?"

"About two minutes ago!"

"I thought that darned dog would recognize me," Ben muttered, "but there was no dealing with him out there."

Apollo stayed close as Dr. Dave found the hammer and nails he needed to do a rough repair on the door casing. Afterwards, Apollo followed his newfound master back up the stairs and into the apartment. He walked over as Dr. Dave sat on the edge of the bed.

"Well, you big lug," Dr. Dave said as he petted Apollo's head and ruffled up his ears, "you sure earned your grub this week. You could come in handy around this place after all."

Apollo rooted his nose under Dr. Dave's hand and moaned as he got his forehead rubbed.

"If you're going to stay around here," Dr. Dave continued, "we'll have to come up with a name for you."

Apollo sat attentively staring up at Dr. Dave.

"How about – Lug? What do you think of that name, boy?"

Apollo's look of sheer satisfaction was his answer. It was obvious that as long as he got his quota of attention, he could care less what Dr. Dave called him.

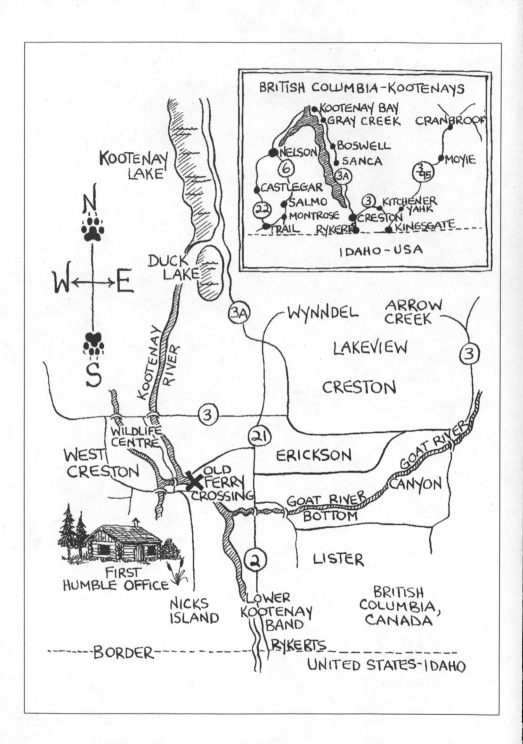

About the Author

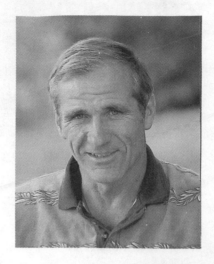

D ave Perrin was raised in Casino, a small town nestled in the hills near Trail, British Columbia. He attended Selkirk College in Castlegar, the University of British Columbia, and the Western College of Veterinary Medicine at Saskatoon, Saskatchewan.

He graduated as a veterinarian in 1973 and practiced in the Creston Valley until 1998. After a year in Hawaii where he began writing the first book about the profession he loved, he returned to his farm in Lister, BC. He established Dave's Press and has published five books on his veterinary adventures: *Don't Turn Your Back in the Barn* (2000), *Dr. Dave's Stallside Manner* (2001), *Where Does it Hurt?* (2003), *Never Say Die* (2006) and *When the Going Gets Tough* (2010). In 2004 Dave's Press published a book about a young girl growing up in the fundamentalist Latter Day Saint community of Bountiful called *Keep Sweet…Children of Polygamy*.

Dr Perrin continued to write and practice veterinary medicine as a locum in British Columbia until a car accident in June of 2009 in which he suffered a broken neck and partial paralysis of his right arm. Although his practice career has been curtailed by a loss of sensation in his right hand, he continues to write.